"BARTHOLOMEW GILL'S NOVELS ARE QUITE A BIT MORE THAN POLICE PROCEDURALS...THEY ARE DISTINGUISHED BY THE QUIRKY INTEGRITY THAT MAKES McGARR A VIVID INDIVIDUAL, BY GILL'S ABILITY TO RENDER THE EVERYDAY SPEECH OF DUBLIN AS MUSIC, AND BY THE PASSIONS SO KEENLY FELT BY HIS CHARACTERS ON BOTH SIDES OF THE LAW."
*Detroit News*

# DEATH ON A COLD, WILD RIVER

"This well-turned plot highlights the rugged vibrancy and anachronisms of Ireland and its citizens without ever succumbing to cliched Emerald Isle sentimentality."
*Publishers Weekly*

# DEATH OF A JOYCE SCHOLAR

"Sings with an Irish lilt...
Clever, witty, intellectually challenging, tender and sad"
*Washington Post Book World*

"A rich, grand book"
*Denver Post*

# THE DEATH OF LOVE

"Strikingly intelligent...Devilishly intricate"
*The New York Times Book Review*

"Wonderful...Fascinating...
I haven't had this much fun since—
well, since Sherlock Holmes."
*Los Angeles Times*

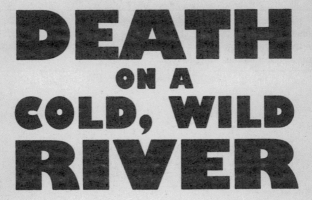

# DEATH
## ON A
# COLD, WILD
# RIVER

### A PETER McGARR MYSTERY

# BARTHOLOMEW GILL

AVON BOOKS  NEW YORK

AVON BOOKS
A division of
The Hearst Corporation
1350 Avenue of the Americas
New York, New York 10019

Published in hardcover by William Morrow and Company, Inc.; for information address Permissions Department, William Morrow and Company, Inc., 1350 Avenue of the Americas, New York, New York 10019.

First Avon Books Printing: August 1994

# PART I

The people of the cities have the machine, which is prose and a *parvenu*. They have few events. They can turn over the incidents of a long life as they sit by the fire. With us, nothing has time to father meaning, and too many things are occurring for ever a big heart to hold.

—W. B. YEATS

# 1

# Rising to the Bait

It was a night Nellie Millar could die for. And did. She had arrived at the mouth of the Owenea River near Ardara in South Donegal, where she lived, to fish for the salmon that were now entering the river. From time to time she could see them, their silver sides flashing through the tannin-rich, amber water. Some were leaping out of pure delight and exuberance—the sight always made her think—to have returned to where they had been hatched.

Sure, she could walk back to the Land Rover in the car park, rig her rod, and climb into her waders. With a Lemon and Gray salmon fly, a Thunder and Lightning, or even a classic Jock Scot—all of which she had dressed herself in her tiny fly-tying shop in town—Nellie might with luck attract several of the fish and have what was known locally as "a good night on the river."

But the big salmon, the smart salmon, the trophy salmon that had spawned in the Owenea before would remain in the headwaters of Loughros More Bay until flood tide, and then dart, like lightning, to the third or fourth lying pool beyond the bridge.

One of them was what Nellie was after. A certain trophy taken when the river was at its crest. To silence her critics, the most trenchant of whom had said in *Eire Rod & Reel*:

Nellie Millar indeed practices the *gentle art*, as perhaps no other woman has since Dame Juliana Berners, whose self-described exploits in the sixteenth century are accounted apocryphal by some. What remains to be proven is that Millar can fish strong waters and catch big fish.

It is one thing to be declared (by this journal, for which she once worked) "the best fisher bar none in all of Ireland." It is quite another to land sizable quarry on a major, formidable confluence where, of course, the truly noble fish lie.

Netting a full creel on a chalk stream or in a quiet lake is no proof of the competence that some have claimed for Millar. It is rumored that she fears swift water, even in her own Owenea when it is in spate. Perhaps the most challenging fishing grounds should best be left to men.

Which was true—her fear of strong water. Beyond the obvious sexist bias of the piece, it was what galled her most. As a child while fishing with her father, they had both nearly been swept from the mouth of the Bandon River, when the tide had risen and suddenly she had found herself caught by the current.

Since that time, Nellie had remained nearly phobic about rips and freshets and places, like this, where the bottom suddenly dropped off, and she could lose her footing on the granite pebbles that were as slick as greased ball bearings in the swift current. And drown. Tonight she would confront that fear, and silence her critics.

And what an evening it was, unusual for late July with a sharp onshore breeze gusting in off the ocean to the west. There towering cloud masses, limned by the setting sun, looked like the backdrop of a stage set from some epic saga—say, the Fenian tales.

The frame on one side of the bay was Slieve Tooey, the tallest ocean headland in all of Europe. The other side presented a ten-mile expanse of lush green fields, rock walls, and neat white cottages sloping up to the lesser eminence of Dunmore Head.

Because of white sand shallows, the water of the bay was a brilliant turquoise color. The ocean beyond was deep blue, almost black, its rollers fringed with whitecaps. In all, "fierce beautiful," as her dear, recently dead mother had said about this part of Ireland; Donegal could be cruel and dangerous in other seasons.

Yet it was a setting that Nellie believed she could look at forever without tiring. She had settled here nearly eleven years earlier after a successful career writing for various sport fishing magazines, mainly in North America. Love of two kinds had brought her back to Ireland—for a man, who had an equally unlikely career based in Dublin, and for this river in South Donegal that she compared (always favorably) to the Spey in Scotland.

It was nearly dark now, and the flood tide in full roiling spate. Nellie rose and walked back to the Rover to begin the challenge that had been set her. Her companion (who would be her witness) was nowhere to be seen, but her gear had been laid out, and a stout leader and strong tippet were fixed to her line.

Nellie quickly doffed her Wellies, stepped into her chest waders, and clasped the flotation belt. Clinched tight around her waist, the belt would keep any water that flowed up over the bib from invading the legs of the boots. In such a way the waders would act like balloons and keep her at least somewhat buoyant, should she lose her footing.

Nellie added a hooded, waterproof fishing jacket, before glancing in the side mirror of the Rover. At fifty-four Nellie Millar was still a pretty woman whose white-blond hair— streaked with age but also bleached from the sun—was braided and tied at the back of her head. Her skin, however, had not fared as well.

After three decades of exposure to wind and sun, it was now creased and leathery. Yet it was a golden color that rather complemented her hair and for which she was grateful. At least she was not mottled red, like so many others of the fishing tribe. Also, because she had been active and had had no children, she had kept her figure. In all she was pleased with how she had aged.

She banged shut the door, and a flock of crows, rising in a cluster of villainy from a nearby oak, let loose a chorus of lugubrious cackles. Nellie checked her watch; it was nearly 11:00. Rod and wading staff in hand, she set out.

From the top of the stile of the wall by the bridge, Nellie could hear that the river had changed even during the short period of time it had taken her to change into her fishing gear. She paused to listen to its angry roar.

Five days earlier an Atlantic storm had swept in from the south off the Gulf Stream. It had brought rain that had increased in intensity until, on the third day, the pounding tempest had flooded fields and made low-lying roads impassable. The scenario, however, could not be more perfect for salmon to enter in the Owenea.

The fish required a high water level and relatively warm temperatures to begin their trek up the rocky and precipitous river, and conditions had seldom been better. The catchment area of the Owenea was immense, draining mountains as distant as Knockrawer and Croveenanta some twenty and thirty miles away; the spate would continue now for a week.

Cloaked in deeper darkness, the riverbank was muddy, and Nellie made her way with slow, cautious steps, mindful of the stiff breeze that buffeted her. She passed by the first pool where, now and then, she could see salmon jumping, and also the second. Because of their strength, the big fish would have been able to fight the deluge and would now be resting in the fourth pool, which was called the "Big Hole." It was wide, extraordinarily deep, and less swift. They would wait there until first light before moving on.

Nellie enjoyed fishing for most types of game fish—trout, pike, bass, bonefish, sea trout—but to her mind the salmon was the premier catch. An anadromous species, salmon were hatched in fresh water, where they spent most of a year at least before migrating downstream to the sea. There they passed a full seawinter (and sometimes up to four) before returning to spawn. Now they would be brimming with a strength that only constant feeding on rich capelin and shrimp could impart.

Just entering the river, their sides were a shiny, nearly phosphorescent, silver color and their flesh a deep characteristic red, courtesy of all the shrimp they had consumed. Once back in fresh water, however, the salmon would not—in fact, *could* not—feed, because their digestive tracts had adapted physiologically to a marine environment.

Thus, salmon had to be *lured* literally into feeding. The bait had to be so attractive and presented with such perfection that it could overwhelm their distaste. And therein lay the sport—at least for Nellie—of creating with her own hands out of an assortment of line, feathers, hackle, hair, and hooks, fly patterns that would goad the fish into rising to her bait. And in placing that bait where it would be certain to command their attention. Also, there was the reward of the catch itself; Nellie enjoyed *eating* fresh, sea-bright salmon nearly as much as netting them ashore.

From the dark bank of the river, she now set about casting a Lemon and Gray. It was her own interpretation of a popular Irish pattern that had long been successful on the Owenea and was, she knew from experience, well suited to night fishing in the turbid spate river.

Stripping some line from the reel, Nellie began whipping the fifteen-foot, two-handed rod back and forth, roughly from the position ten on the clock back to two, gradually adding more and more line to the airborne loop, until the fly could reach the pool where the big fish would be lying. On her final swing forward, she added a surfeit of line to compensate for the stiff breeze. The Lemon and Gray sailed off into the darkness and fell at a forty-five degree angle downstream. From there it would be carried to the edge of the pool.

Nellie also played it a bit, twitching the end of the rod and stripping in the line with her left hand. The point— some experts claimed—was to make the fly resemble a small, bright, injured fish. In the ocean, which the salmon had just left, they of needs had been voracious feeders, since during cool, dry spawning seasons they might be forced to remain in the river up to nine months without feeding before conditions were right to procreate. By then their skins would be dark, their flesh white and tasteless, and only a few would survive to breed again.

Which was why it was best to catch them now when they were fresh, Nellie thought.

On her third cast to the same spot, she believed she felt a tug, though it might have been a riffle, and she snubbed her forefinger against the line, waiting before she stripped it back.

But nothing. Because of the wind and the spate condition of the Owenea, she just wasn't managing to reach the middle of the pool. She could reel in the line and walk back the way she had come to the bridge and cross over to the other side. But fishing from the opposite bank would put her between the river and the moon, and might spook the salmon; also she would waste at least a half hour. The option was to fish from the stream.

Slowly, cautiously, she sat on the bank and then, feeling for the bottom with her wading staff, which was attached to her left wrist by a leather thong, she let down her legs into the swirling eddies in the lee of the bank. Even through the insulation of the waders and her flannel trousers she immediately felt the chill of the frigid water that had flowed into the river from high mountain sources.

Again she probed the depths before taking another step toward the pool. And another, until the water was up to her thighs. She had to lean upstream, the current was so strong.

But satisfied that she could hold the position without the aid of the staff, Nellie repeated the procedure—casting thrice on a forty-five degree angle and letting the current carry the Lemon and Gray down into the pool.

Nearly a half hour passed in such a way, with the level of the Owenea still rising and the moon becoming obscured behind a dense cloud bank. Nellie was now perhaps a half mile from the bridge and the car park, and she had just decided that she had guessed wrong and would have to wait for some other night for a trophy fish. It was then, on her final cast, that the moon suddenly appeared from behind the clouds and the fly struck the edge of the pool.

The fish did not wait for it to sink. Nor did it strike with the force and bravado of a grilse (a one-seawinter salmon), which characteristically erupted from the depths to seize a fly and splash back into the pool. Instead Nellie saw only the silver side and back of the salmon as it rolled over in the moonlight, took the fly into its mouth, and sank again. But what a back! There was at least four feet of it, and its tail was the size of a shovel.

Unlike when fishing for other species, Nellie did not immediately pull back the rod to set the hook. Rather, she waited while the fish stripped line from her reel—not fast, no run—just a slow, steady, strong (she could feel its power in the rod) movement through the stiff current to the far edge of the deep pool.

Then there came the pause when, Nellie always imagined, a salmon was trying to determine what it had in its mouth, which was soft and slick. A hook had to pierce the mucous membrane before it could be set. It was then that she said, "Good evening, Madame Salmon," as she had been taught by her father some forty years before, and she simply snubbed down the line and tightened the butt of the rod against her stomach. In such a way, when the salmon now began moving again, it hooked itself. And the battle was joined.

Its leap was spectacular; like a great silver emanation— a missile, a geyser—it burst from the depths. In the moonlight it wriggled and twisted, shedding water and foam, and struggled with all its stored strength to shake the hook from its jaw. Like a boulder it splashed back into the pool.

Nellie rejoiced and quickly slacked off, so the momentum of the salmon's fall would not snap the line. She did not know if she had caught a trophy fish, but she had surely caught a fish large enough to prove the point that she could and did fish strong waters for big fish, *if* she could get it in. Which with the Owenea in full spate was a challenge more difficult by far than simply *hooking* a big fish.

"When it pulls, you don't. When it doesn't, you do." Again it was her father's advice; he had taught her early and well.

Dutifully Nellie now took in line as the salmon drifted downstream with the current; she would have to wait to see what the fish would do. Seconds went by. A minute. Two. It was a big, strong, *smart* fish.

If it turned and fled with the current back toward the bridge and the sea, there would be little that she could do; she only had two hundred yards of backing and the combined weight of the salmon, the speed of its charge, and the flow of the river would certainly break the twelve-pound-test, tippet line. And any pressure now on the line from upstream would only make it flee seaward.

Also, Nellie was much deeper into the Owenea than she had planned to venture, nearly up to her ribs. Even here in an eddy where the current was less severe, she was having trouble maintaining her footing in the shifting mounds of rounded stones and mossy boulders. With both hands on the rod and without recourse to the wading staff, she was slipping, and she kept having to reposition her feet, which required a precarious kind of jog-in-place.

She glanced up at the bank, hoping her companion was about. She didn't know how she would ever net, tail, or gaff the fish, should she be able to bring it up beside her. All three devices (net, tailer, and gaff) were attached to the back of her fishing jacket.

It was only then that she realized what she had been feeling at the back of her waders for some time now. Water, and plenty of it. *Why*, when the waders were almost new and had been water-filled-tested, or so the manufacturer claimed?

From somewhere at the small of her back, it was now pouring into her legs, filling the boots, and pulling her down into the shifting mounds of granite pebbles. Nellie tried to lift one leg and nearly couldn't; already the waders were filled with a great volume of water.

The salmon leaped again—upstream; at least that was something—and began a strong run toward the opposite bank, darting up through the current toward the pool where it had been hooked.

Nellie reeled in as much line as she thought judicious, and then, wedging the butt of the pole under her right arm, reached around her waist with the left to assay the cause of the leak. A tear, rather, a clean rip in the very back of the waders just under the cinched belt.

But—*how*? The waders had been perfect, she was certain, when she had left her shop for her tea that evening. And she had neither fallen nor caught them on anything. It was a fallacy that sodden waders could pull you down, but in such conditions they would probably make it impossible to emerge from the river without help or pulling them off first.

Passing beyond the pool, the salmon now began lunging, in and out of the water, its back breaking the surface like a dolphin. The pole squirted from under Nellie's arms, and without thinking of the consequences she grabbed for it with both hands. She lost her footing and was pulled out into the rip of the current. It plucked her up, like so much flotsam, and swirled her downstream.

She could now feel the remaining trapped air rushing from the waders, and she tried to decide what to do—release the pole and the fish and with the wading staff try to push herself back toward the riverbank? But then what? Maybe she could uncinch the belt and free herself from the waders—no, they were also strapped to her shoulders, and she would first have to unzip and unsnap the fishing jacket, which would require two hands.

At least now the pole, the line, and the fish—like a kind of sea anchor—were slowing her drift downstream and keeping her afloat. But at the same time she was swinging out into the middle of the swollen river.

It was then that the line broke, and Nellie went under for the first time—tumbling, swirling head over heels. She was smashed into one submerged boulder, held for a moment, and then hurled at another.

She released the pole and then madly, frantically fought to get hold of the wading staff, which was flailing in the current. Maybe she could use it to push herself to the surface.

"Help!" she shouted, when in a rapid she suddenly discovered her head out of water. Her feet had become wedged into a crevice of a rock ledge, with the entire weight of the river pouring over her back. "Help! I'm over here! I'm drowning!" she again called out into the darkness; it was no time for false pride.

With all her strength she tried to keep the river from pushing her downstream, but she knew she could not endure. Her legs were quaking, quivering, and she was allowed just one more breath before she was washed from the ledge and back into the depths.

There she bounced off the bottom and tumbled again and again. Every once in a while, when she thought her lungs would burst, she managed to push herself off the bottom, up to the surface for another breath until, with a jarring crash that split her scalp and sent a bolt of pain from her shoulder down and into her right hand, she slammed full force against the pier of the rock bridge over the road.

"Help!" she gasped, snapping her head up to squint into the darkness in hopes that her companion or somebody—*anybody*—would be there to save her.

And . . . could she be imagining it? No—there *was* a figure leaning over the rail, silhouetted against the moonlit sky. "Help! Help me, please—I'm drowning." She tried to grasp and raise the wading staff, which was still attached to her wrist by its leather thong. The river was so high that a person, reaching down, could seize it. But her fingers were too cold or too weak or injured, and if she let go with the other hand, she would be swept past the bridge and out to sea.

"Please!" she implored. "Do something, throw me something! Your jacket, a stick, *anything*!" She knew she would not be able to keep hold of the cold, slippery stones of the pier for much longer.

But the figure above her did not stir. Instead of his help, she heard him shout,

> "She lifts her silver gills above the flood,
> And greedily sucks in th' unfaithful food."

What? Nellie had heard—no—she had *read* that before. It was the first couplet of a poem that had been sent to an environmental newsletter that Nellie helped to edit, and she had published it in the "Mailbag" column. The accompanying letter condemned sport fishing for salmon as a pastime of the "idle rich, both domestic and foreign, who are seeking to deprive traditional Irish fishermen of their livelihoods so they can disport themselves at their leave."

### Death on a Cold, Wild River

> "She roils, and writhes her straining body round,
> Then headlong shoots beneath the dashing tide."

Twisting her head up to him once more, Nellie begged, "Please—please *help* me!"
The figure did not move.

> "Now in the burden'd stream she sinking lies,
> Stretches her quivering arms, and gasping dies."

Nellie turned her face to the dark wet stones of the pier and sobbed, knowing she could not hold on for much longer. Her other arm was useless, either broken or the shoulder dislocated. "Help me," she sobbed. "Please, help me."

Nellie did not see the gob of phlegm that was spat at her from above.

A few moments later her right hand slid across the face of the pier, and the rip of the flood through the bridge arches closed over her head.

Distancing herself from her own death as she swirled down the river toward Loughros More Bay and began to choke, Nellie decided that whoever it had been on the bridge was right. How many fish had she pulled out of their natural medium into the sickening air? Thousands.

And here she was fittingly being pulled into the sickening flood.

But how many more thousands he?

# 2

# On Pity and Fear

Peter McGarr learned of the death of Nellie Millar two nights later while sitting in the study of his home in Rathmines, a suburb of Dublin.

He was explaining the comics to his daughter and only child, Madeleine, who was three years old, when out of the corner of his eye he saw his wife snap down the newspaper. She stared at him for a while, then raised it in front of her again.

The McGarrs had been married eleven years, and he knew what it meant. She had read some distressing bit of news, but had decided to keep it from him. For his own sake.

Of late McGarr had troubles of his own that were involved with his work as Chief Superintendent of the Serious Crimes Unit of the Garda Siochana, the Irish police. He was currently suspended pending a Tribunal of Enquiry that was looking into a number of events that had culminated in the assassination of a Taosieach seven months earlier.

"What is it?" he asked.

"Ah, nothing." Her voice was thick with emotion.

McGarr studied the back of the page and decided she was reading the obituary column. "I'll only be reading it myself."

"Yah."

He heard a sniffle, and a hand left an edge of the paper for a moment.

Maddie pointed to the funny page, saying, "Read this one, Daddy."

McGarr did, and, when he glanced up again, the newspaper was still in front of Noreen's face. "Well?"

"Sure—it'll only ruin the moment. Work away at what you're doing."

"I can't now. You've got my interest up."

When Noreen lowered the paper, her well-made features were distorted by sorrow. Nearly twenty years younger than he, she was a trim, pretty woman, with precise features and red hair. The observation was not new, but McGarr had noted in the past that redheads cried best. Or worst. The lids of Noreen's light green eyes were now scarlet, her face looked puffy, and her usually strong mouth was a twisted line. In all, a tragic mask. "Oh, Peter—Nellie Millar has died."

It took a moment for the news to sink in. McGarr then lowered Maddie to the floor, the child suddenly somber to see her mother crying. "How?"

"A 'misadventure,' they're calling it. She was fishing her Owenea in spate. She got in over her head, they assume, and was swept away."

"*In* the Owenea?" McGarr asked. Nobody got into the Owenea to fish, especially when it was in spate. The Owenea could be a vicious river; there were holes in it fathoms deep. And certainly not Nellie Millar, who was as knowledgeable a fisher as there was, most particularly about the Owenea, which she "owned," as was said in fishing circles.

"Here, read it yourself." Noreen stood and handed him the paper, then walked toward the door to the hallway, Maddie following.

While reading the notice, McGarr himself moved out of the study and into his den at the other end of the Georgian structure. It was the room he repaired to whenever he was preoccupied.

Peter McGarr was a short, stocky man in his early fifties whose nose had been broken more than once and was a bit angled to one side. Bald now, he allowed the hair that remained on the sides of his head to curl at the nape of his neck; it was red—like his wife's and his daughter's. Recently he had begun to put on weight, but the impression of solidity and strength had not diminished. Nor the intensity in his light gray eyes.

Tonight he was wearing a silk smoking jacket in a tasteful floral pattern with tuxedo lapels. It was a present from Noreen, who owned a picture gallery in fashionable Dawson Street, and was always trying to improve his wardrobe, which was largely utilitarian. Beneath the jacket he was wearing the white shirt and trousers to the iron-gray suit he had worn that day to the Tribunal. He sat in his favorite chair.

The paper said little more than Noreen had told him, mentioning that Nellie had left only her father and listing the dates and hours of viewing and burial in Ardara, County Donegal, in the far northwest of the country.

It would probably kill Nelson Millar was McGarr's first thought. He was well advanced in age now—how old? Seventy-five at least—and Nellie had been his only child, in fact, all the family he possessed, his wife having been taken some three years earlier.

McGarr thought of how he had first met Nelson Millar, and how the man had influenced his life. And of Nellie, whom McGarr had nearly married, more time out of mind now than McGarr chose to consider.

Sixteen years ago to be exact. McGarr had then only recently returned to Ireland after fourteen years of working first for the French police and later for Interpol, also on the Continent. He had become interested in salmon fishing one evening when he cast a mayfly into a pool where he knew a fat trout was lying.

The fly had not quite touched down when the gently flowing surface of the river exploded with the flash of an eight-pound, sea-bright grilse. It was that ecstatic moment in angling when a fish that you've conjured from the depths appears, as if to salute and challenge you, and the struggle is on.

With a light-action rod and light tackle, it took McGarr all of his accumulated knowledge of trout fishing, at least a half hour, and no little luck to land the fish. And, equally with the salmon, McGarr was hooked. For life.

A week later and fully equipped, McGarr found himself on the shores of Lough Eske in Donegal where, he had heard, salmon had arrived and a ghillie might be engaged. The man had no phone, and thus McGarr arrived at a small cottage, overlooking the picturesque lake, unannounced, only to discover that the ghillie had already been hired, in fact for the week. No other ghillies were available. Even so, he was invited in for tea with the ghillie and the man who had already claimed his service.

Nelson Millar was then a tall man of middle age with patrician features and a soft, melodious voice that only hinted at his origins in County Mayo. Over tea he spoke with McGarr about this and that, gradually learning without direct inquiry that McGarr was new to salmon fishing but had fished for trout, tied his own flies, and was possibly adept at catching that species.

But mostly—McGarr only later realized—Nelson Millar had been interested in knowing if McGarr was a sportsman: somebody who fished out of love of the sport and out of respect and perhaps even reverence for nature. At length he said, "Why don't you join us today, Peter. There's rough water in the lough, and I'll fish for a while," and you can watch me and learn, went unsaid, "and then you'll fish." And be taught.

"A grand idea," agreed the ghillie, warming to the prospect of a double fee and the possibility of putting a strong, young back into the oars, should conditions worsen.

And so their friendship began, Millar acting the part of informal mentor: pointing out the conditions of a lake or stream, imparting to McGarr his vast knowledge of the natural world, showing him the signs of where fish lay and how to take them or let them go. Nelson categorically would never keep a smallish grilse, a hen salmon on her spawn run, or any kelt (a salmon returning to the sea). Yet in spite of his rigid practice fishing, Millar was dogmatic about nothing else. In fact, he was good company—the very best by McGarr's standard—since he brought to a conversation not only good stories but the credibility that only accurate detail could impart.

Those same details were his daughter Nellie's stock-in-trade. She sportfished for a living, writing about it biweekly in *The Irish Times* from Clarks Fork in the Yellowstone, from Patagonia, from the rivers of the Pyrenees, among other intriguing venues. It was plain to McGarr that she had learned to fish from her father. Equally obvious, however, was her talent; she could write about fishing in a manner that was engaging. McGarr had read her column avidly even before he had met her father.

Meeting her finally was something else. At first he thought she must be some older sister, when he saw her out on the lawn of her father's house in Foxford, casting what turned out to be a new-model blank line. The picture of her in *The Times* was reduced and, he supposed, was a dated file photo. Also, whenever her name had been mentioned in conversation, her father only ever smiled and said, "Nellie's a good girl." And no more.

In McGarr's estimation, however, Nellie was no girl. Rather, she was a beautiful *woman*. She was almost exactly his age and had a forthright yet witty manner that he found disarming. "My father tells me you're the new Nelligan," she said, meaning Superintendent Brian Nelligan, a notorious former head of Special Branch who, after the revolution, ruthlessly pursued and was said to have murdered renegade IRA gunmen. "Of salmon, of course."

"Entrapment," McGarr had replied. "That's my game. Salmon, trout, pike—actually, *wild* life of any sort."

"Do you mean, of the two-legged kind?"

McGarr had nodded. "When I'm lucky. I understand you've been on safari. How d'*you* do?"

And from that moment the "crack"—as was said in Ireland about scintillating conversation and good times—was on. Nellie Millar was a diminutive blond woman with a lithe, athletic build and curiously dark eyes. Her mother had been "black" Irish, and consequently her skin, which had been much-exposed to sun and wind, was a deep, sheeny brown and her hair sun-streaked almost white.

In all the effect was rather startling and certainly attractive, at least to McGarr. The feature he liked best about the physical Nellie Millar, however, was her shoulders

# Death on a Cold, Wild River

which were so square they felt knobbed under his hands. McGarr had occasion to admire them, since not long after their first meeting, Nellie and he became lovers of the most passionate sort, whenever they could be together, which was the difficulty. They had little opportunity, the demands of their separate careers keeping them apart.

Finally Nellie and he understood that one of them would have to make some concession to the relationship, were it to continue. Nellie decided she would quit the magazine and set up a fly-fishing shop and school, based in Ardara on the Owenea. It would be aimed at women who wished to learn fly-fishing.

During their long separations, she had also written a book, *Juliana Revisited*, extolling the calming virtues of the sport along with anecdotes of her own experience among the fly-fishing "fraternity," as it was known. In the book she made—to McGarr's mind—the blatantly sexist point that women, being more dexterous and careful than men, might prove themselves far better fly-fishers, since, "From the tying of flies, through the casting of them, to the landing of game fish, the sport requires more precision than strength or brute force." McGarr remembered the last two words.

The book was widely praised, sold well, and entered the lexicon of fishing literature. How-to and fishing-holiday videos for single women followed, to say nothing of money. With it, Nellie established herself in Ardara, buying her fly shop and what McGarr thought of as a magnificent house right in town overlooking Loughros More Bay. Almost to the day that McGarr met Noreen. A decade ago.

Since that time McGarr had spent only one painful afternoon with Nellie, though he had continued to fish with her father both in spring and fall. Always the gentleman, the older man never mentioned Nellie to him, but McGarr suspicioned he knew.

McGarr now glanced at the phone, thinking he should ring up Nelson. But the viewing was on the morrow, which would be better. In person. He would have to get an early start, Ardara being a good six-hour drive.

At that moment Maddie peeked her bright head around the corner of the door and peered at McGarr, as though to assess his mood. Emboldened, she took another step and squared herself in the doorway. She then clasped her hands behind her back in an exact copy of the pose he sometimes assumed when pondering something difficult. His daughter and only child. The image of himself and the wife he loved.

He thought of all the joy and hope and laughter she had brought into his life, and what he would do—how he could possibly go on!—without her.

Poor Nelson Millar! How would he get through it all? With McGarr's help, of course, and that of his and Nellie's many friends, McGarr hoped.

And what else was McGarr feeling? Guilt for having treated Nellie so shabbily. After telling her that he planned to marry somebody else, she had said, "I suppose she's a younger woman."

McGarr had nodded.

"How much younger?"

"Younger."

"Ten years? Twenty?"

"Twenty."

Nellie shook her head. "I misjudged *us*."

The last time McGarr had seen her.

"Mammy *stopped* crying," Maddie now said.

It was only then that McGarr remembered Noreen's tears, and he was touched by her concern. She had not known Nellie, who in a way had been her rival, and she had only met Nelson once. But she knew of McGarr's history with Nellie, since she had made him tell her, and her sorrow—he guessed—was for him. To have lost somebody who had been so much of his life at one time.

Noreen now appeared behind Maddie with a bottle and two glasses. "Would this help?"

McGarr shook his head and blotted the corners of his eyes with the cuffs of his shirtsleeves. Him, the former head of the Murder Squad and reputed by criminals and colleagues alike to be one of the hardest men in the country.

He then held out his arms so Maddie could run to him. Drawing her to his breast, he was again riven by the fear he had felt earlier. He hoped he never lived to see his daughter die.

"Nelson," he murmured.

# 3

# Wake Spark

Ardara sits at the head of Loughros More Bay. Meaning "high ring-fort" in Irish, *Ard an Ratha* was a bastion in ancient times that not only commanded the bay but also controlled transit across a ford in the Owentocker River. Neither overly pretty nor quaint, Ardara was to McGarr's way of thinking one of the most inviting villages in Ireland.

It had something to do with its containment. A tall church bordered each end of the town. Between them was a tight pack of shops and the "Diamond," as it was called— a wide space in front of the Nesbitt Arms Hotel where four roads met. The road north led up a steep hill to a church-yard where one could survey the entire area. Nellie would be buried there, McGarr had read.

Pulling up in front of the hotel, he now wondered how much his enjoyment of Ardara was due to the way Nellie had presented it to him those many years ago—like a gift. It was as though she had said, I have come back to Ireland,

and it is here that I—and, I hope, we—can live. At the time it had seemed a pleasant prospect, and with her McGarr had met the locals, who were a friendly lot. He had helped Nellie negotiate the purchase of both of her properties—the fly-tying shop by the bridge and the house where she was now being waked.

It was so large that McGarr knew that her father would insist on his staying there. But he did not wish to burden the older man unduly in his time of woe, and selfishly he was not sure he could pass a quiet night in a place that contained so many memories. Thus McGarr secured lodgings at the Nesbitt Arms, and, contrary to what he knew was good form, tried to steel himself with several large whiskeys in the bar.

But it was no use. He had to force his sturdy legs to carry him through the gate that said LEIXLIP—"Salmon-Leap" from the Norse *lax*, meaning salmon. His heart was still in his throat.

Nelson Millar was standing near the door, welcoming people, and McGarr was surprised by how unchanged he always remained. Like McGarr's own father, he was one of those men who, at some stage of early middle age, seem to keep that general appearance into their seventies. There might be some diminution of the hairline or a slight narrowing of the face, but overall he still looked like the man McGarr had met in the ghillie's cottage all those years ago.

Millar was tall and thin with the good shoulders that he had given Nellie. His silver hair was thin on top but neatly trimmed and combed back on the sides of his head. His face was square, but his features were sharp with a protrusive upper lip and a strong chin. He was still a handsome man.

Semiretired now, he spent most of his time out-of-doors,

and in the summer, like now, his skin was a bronze color. He was wearing a deep blue, pin-striped suit, a plain blue tie, and there was even a white silk handkerchief folded neatly in his breast pocket. For a widower who had just lost the only family he would ever have, he stood there a testament to considered living.

Behind him in the room, gathered by a drinks table, was a group of somewhat younger men whom McGarr recognized as people who fished with Nelson. There were others scattered about the large room. Locals come to pay their respects, McGarr suspected.

"Peter!" said Nelson Millar in an intense whisper. "I was hoping you'd come." He took McGarr's hand in both of his, his eyes overbright. McGarr had seen the effect before; it was emotional shock. Only later, perhaps days or weeks from now, would the reality of his daughter's death hit him.

"Of course, Nelson. I don't know how to tell you how—" McGarr began to say before the older man mercifully cut him off.

"I know, I know. I would have liked her to have lived to a ripe old age, but she died doing what she loved best." It was his public statement, McGarr judged, that would ease the grief of others. A true gentle man, Nelson was carrying on decorously, and he would mourn his daughter in private. Later. "Are you staying for the funeral?"

McGarr nodded and put pressure on the man's hand. "I'll be here."

"Have a drink, and I'll join you in a moment. Nellie's over there. Will you look at the flowers? I didn't realize how many friends she had. They're pouring in from all over the world."

Slowly McGarr weaved his way through the other mourners, not wanting to see what he was about to see—Nellie, the lively one, perhaps the most vigorous person he had ever known. Dead.

It was far worse than he could have imagined. Only on the rarest of occasions could he remember having seen Nellie wearing a dress. Even for television interviews she had dressed no more formally than khakis and a jumper. But here she was garbed in a long black dress made of something like velveteen with a lace collar and more at the cuffs.

And whatever the undertaker had tried to do with her weathered skin was ghastly. He had applied powder, rouge, and makeup with a trowel, it seemed, even to the backs of her hands, which were gathered at her waist. In the attempt to . . . what? Make her look more feminine and ladylike? After the ultimate indignity, here was yet another.

And still it was the Nellie that McGarr had known and with whom he had spent so much free—in the best sense—time: days out on rivers and lakes, saying little but listening much, and putting themselves in touch with the vitality of the earth, of which Nellie had been so much a part. There had been a spark in her that few could equal, and perhaps in that way marriage—to McGarr or to anybody—would have damped it, marriage being a certain submission for both parties.

The Millars were Church of Ireland, and a rail was provided. McGarr was not a religious man in the practicing sense, but he believed in life and its possibilities, and he would pray to that . . . spark—formerly in her, in him, and in the universe.

When he arose, he was handed a drink by one of the men whom Nelson fished with. They were then joined by the others who, in Irish style, mourned Nellie by recounting the best that they had known of her. Thin stuff, McGarr judged, compared to what he had shared with her, which was either beyond telling or would have been inappropriate to relate. Instead he only nodded and agreed. And raised his glass.

At length the others began to depart, agreeing to meet later at the hotel bar. It was then McGarr moved toward the mantel. There to one side of the clock was a picture of him standing on the banks of the Moy, Ireland's most productive salmon river, with four fat salmon glinting silver in the sun by his feet.

Wearing a slicker, McGarr was grasping a fly rod, and the smile on his face was perhaps the fullest that had ever been snapped of him. Yet in no way could it reveal the joy that he had experienced that day, not only in catching the salmon but in realizing that Nellie and he had "clicked"—the term she later used—by which she meant that they could have fun together and be a pair.

"It was her favorite photograph."

When Nelson Millar did not add "of you," McGarr felt a pang of acute embarrassment. And shame.

Worse when Nelson added, "Why did you not marry her, Peter? It was what she wanted, when she set herself up here in Ardara."

And what was I to do—quit my career, come out here and fish beside her? McGarr could have replied. We were away from each other so much that I met somebody else whom I realized I loved more. And then sometimes things happen quickly, pointedly, terminally between two people, and even after much pleasant, shared experience. They then go their separate ways.

But McGarr only looked down into his empty glass. It was the man's sorrow and anger at the face of his daughter's death that was speaking. And nothing else.

Millar's hand fell on McGarr's shoulder. "Sorry—that was uncalled for. I forgot myself. And, sure, you went through all that years ago, you and Nellie. It's just"—he straightened up to look around the room, as if to make sure that everybody else was gone. "I've got something to show you. I think she could have used your presence. How's your drink? Here, let me fill it for you. I rather need one myself."

After Millar topped up the glasses, he led McGarr upstairs to what McGarr knew was Nellie's bedroom, or at least had been all those years ago when he had helped her move in. "I didn't know what to do with the clothes that she . . . had been wearing when— The mortician returned them to me, and all I could think was that I'd keep the little I had left of Nellie together."

Millar paused, and in the mirror of the dresser McGarr now saw the older man falter as tears came to his eyes. "I mean," he spoke on rapidly, "the question was—what do we clothe her in? I couldn't find anything suitable in here"—he cast a large hand toward the closet, which was open. "And so . . ."

The travesty of the dress, to say nothing of the makeup. McGarr sipped from the glass.

"Only this morning did I get around to sorting out the bundle—shirt, trousers, *waders*." Nelson Millar straightened up and took a long drink from the full glass. When he could speak, he went on. "I hope it's my . . . condition that's making me think this, and not—Peter—look, examine, whatever it is you do . . . and tell me what you see."

McGarr put down his glass and moved toward the chest waders that Nelson had pointed to; it was the first of five pair hanging at the beginning of the deep closet that was devoted to fishing equipment, McGarr could see. There had to be three dozen rods strung on hangers along the walls, most split-bamboo Hardys, the very best.

He carried the waders out to window light and noted immediately that they were new, or at least probably had been before Nellie's "misadventure" in the Owenea. It was a euphemism that always set McGarr's teeth on edge.

Most of the green outer surface was still shiny, and the rubberized material was stiffly supple. But there were rough patches of abrasion where, evidently, the waders had bumped up against the rough granite boulders in the river. McGarr turned them around to look at the back.

The same was true of the other side with one exception. There was a neat slit about four inches long just below and parallel to the line of the cinch belt that clasped the waist tight. It was a slice, really, which had cleanly penetrated the rubberized outer layer, the canvaslike substructure of the waders, and also the layer of the insulation beyond.

Could it have been made by some of the litter that most Irish rivers swept from their banks when in spate, he wondered—made after she had drowned, when her body was submerged and being knocked about in the torrent?

The slice was straight. No, *ruler* straight, and so hard by the line of the cinch belt as to be obscured by it. A shard of glass from, say, a broken bottle would have to have been straight and very sharp to have made the cut. More like window glass or perhaps thicker, plate glass. Perhaps her body got trapped for a time in some eddy or whirlpool and rocked back and forth until the jagged edge penetrated. McGarr did not think so—it was too perfect.

"Would there be an empty bottle around?"

The older man had to think for a moment; it was plain that he was now feeling both the whiskey and his sorrow. He looked suddenly drained, and his pale blue eyes were streaked with red. "On the drinks table down in the sitting room, I reckon. And we should be getting back." To Nellie, he meant; in many Irish circles it was bad form to leave the body of a loved one unattended even for the shortest time.

"Do you think we might"— McGarr rejected the word sacrifice—"ruin another pair of these waders?"

"Why not?"

Exactly. McGarr removed a pair that were a duplicate in every way but age—they were well worn.

Down in the kitchen he tapped the bottle on the side of the sink until it cracked then broke. Most of the glass in a river was bottle glass; in all his days fishing he could remember seeing only one pane of window glass that had been trashed on the banks of a river. With his handkerchief McGarr picked up the straightest shard of glass from the bottom of the sink. He glanced at the clock.

Flopping the waders over the cutting board, he held the cinch belt tight, like a straightedge. He then drew the sharp edge of the shattered glass over and back over the material. The rubberized exterior was readily sliced, but he had to saw and saw at the stiff, treated canvas beneath before he managed to cut through it and the foamlike insulation beyond. To complete a full, four-inch gash took another twenty or so seconds. In all, he had spent about a minute sawing vigorously, and the cut was in no way as clean as the incision in the waders Nellie had been found in. McGarr turned his attention back to those.

The cut there was in such a place that, fitting her legs into them in, say, dim light or, say again, under the dome light of a car or van, she would not have noticed the tear. If—say once more—somebody had slit the waders with some sharp instrument, how would he know that Nellie would actually enter the river to fish? The Owenea was not a broad river, and the only possible conditions that

might require wading would be at a large pool when the
river was in spate and casting from the banks could not
place a fly where it was needed near the farther bank.

McGarr removed the broken glass from the sink and
placed it in the bin. With both pairs of waders, he returned
to the sitting room, where Nelson Millar had pulled a chair
close to his daughter's corpse. "There's food"—he waved
to the sideboard—"that all Nellie's friends sent over."

McGarr could tell that the older man was about to go
to pieces altogether, and he would have to speak to him
quickly now that his . . . suspicions? no, his *interest* in exactly how Nellie Millar had died had been aroused. She
had been an enormously experienced fisher and would not
have put herself in danger unduly.

"What about the Guards—do they know about this?"
McGarr meant the local Gardai.

"I only discovered it myself this morning when her . . .
effects were returned."

"Did the undertaker mention a wound on Nellie's lower
back around here?" He pointed to the slit in the waders;
if she had been stabbed, certainly the police would already
have been notified and the body not released. But if the
slicing of the waders had occurred after she had already
donned them and was in the river, certainly whatever had
caused the cut would also have in some way broken her
skin, if only slightly.

Millar shook his head. "Beyond saying she had been
battered by the turbulence, and it took some doing to get
her looking like that." It was plain he didn't care for the
way she looked either, all the makeup and so forth.

McGarr sighed. "I'm afraid I'm going to have to find out.
If you'd care to step out for a moment, Nelson, I'll check."

"Not at all. I'll help you. She was mine too, you know."

There were some wounds in life, McGarr speculated, that

just would never heal. He hoped that Nelson Millar's blaming him for not having married Nellie was not one.

Careful to expose only Nellie's back—and not the always lurid work of embalming—McGarr pulled her over on her side, then zipped down the back of the black velveteen dress. Her once fine, square back was mottled with dun-colored postmortem bruises, but there was no mark at the small of her back, not even so much as a scratch.

Nelson Millar glanced at McGarr. "Then what made the split?"

Or who? "Perhaps you can help me with that."

"Could it have been a ... machine defect?" There was almost a kind of hope in Millar's voice—that there would remain no cloud over his daughter's death, as difficult as it had already been for him.

After they returned her to the original position, McGarr yet again examined the slit in the waders. There was no seam or juncture at that spot to be defective, and the material in that area was fair right up to the cut. Also, if they had been damaged, say, when purchased, Nellie would have noticed the tear. She had been as careful as her father about tackle and accessories.

"What do you know about the night Nellie died, Nelson? Who was she fishing with?"

Seated again, Millar now had a leather-covered notebook in his hand. "I looked to see, after I discovered the slit. As far as I can determine she went out to the Owenea around ten. With the Yank in his Rover. D'you know about the Yank, Peter?" Millar glanced at the table beside McGarr's chair where stood a framed picture. "But then you wouldn't.

"There he is. Nellie met him in Patagonia about a year ago. A younger fella, as you can see. He followed her back here, so. A sycophant, I take him to be. Like a kind of fly-fishing groupie or ... 'wanna-be,' I believe the American term is. Calls himself a 'professional' fly-fisherman, and he writes for various sportfishing magazines from time to time. But—can you imagine?—he doesn't even tie his own flies. He can't. Not a one.

"He tried to pal around with Lee Wulff over in the States, when Wulff was alive. And later Wulff's widow, Joan, who rang Nellie up and warned her against him. It seems he spoke with Joan Wulff about her fishing techniques, then used them as a basis of an article about fishing the Miramichi. Without her permission."

McGarr, of course, knew of the Wulffs, who had been a legendary fishing couple, and of the Miramichi, which was a famous salmon-fishing river in eastern Canada. He picked up the framed photograph.

It pictured Nellie and a darkly handsome young man with sun-streaked hair and full blonding moustache that could not quite disguise what McGarr thought of as a surly mouth—a sculpted, curling upper lip with the smile off to the side. The expression in his light green eyes was triumphant, as he pulled Nellie into the lee of his shoulder. He had conquered her.

Both were wearing fishing gear, and Nellie was raising a hand, seemingly to push a lock of her brilliant hair from her forehead. But the gesture also looked a bit defensive, as if she did not really wish to be snapped like that. And yet she too was smiling and must have placed the picture there in her sitting room for any visitor to see. "Name?"

"Henry 'Hank' Stearns, *fishing* cowboy, he calls himself," Nelson said with distaste. "He can't be more than thirty-two or -three. As I mentioned, she met him down in Argentina where she takes one of her 'classes' every ..." Nelson glanced at the casket. "*Took* a group of well-off women every summer, more as a kind of fantasy trip than for the fishing. They catch fish, mind," he was quick to add. "But why go all that way, unless it's for the scenery."

Or for the snob appeal of saying you fished Patagonia with Nellie Millar, McGarr supposed. "When was that?"

"A year ago. I don't know what went on between them, but he followed her back here. He gave her that picture for her birthday this year. Imagine—a picture of himself and her, as if they were an item."

Her fifty-fourth birthday, McGarr thought, she and he having been the same age nearly to the day. Death had changed that; now Nellie was suddenly as old as the inanimate universe.

"You'll probably think less of me, but I've been prying." Nelson raised the leather notebook in his lap, then opened the volume. "After the waders, I became interested, you see.

"It's Nellie's diary. Of this year. She mentions him now and then—the meeting in Patagonia, then saying they'd been fishing this place and that. The only revealing thing about him and them I could find is this entry. She writes,

> I know I've been missing something in my life for a long time now, but I couldn't decide what it was. Now I know. It is a man. I realize Hank is a bit of a bounder, and he probably has women all over the world. He even admitted to me tonight that he has "a kind of wife" *somewhere*, and children. He wouldn't say how many.
>
> I don't know what my fascination is for him (or his for me, since there's such a difference in our ages, which he doesn't seem to mind. Or ever mention.) It's not love, at least not yet, and certainly not any need for emotional support, since I cherish living on my own and have so many good friends, many of them men, from fishing. I blush to write this but—"

Nelson looked up. "I'm afraid I can't read the rest of this aloud. Too much of a prude, I guess. And then she—" He held out the diary; McGarr reached for it. It took him a while to find the passage, then he read:

> —it's carnal, pure and simple. I didn't think anybody
> could arouse me like that again. Hank's stunningly hand-
> some, of course, and he's like a kind of man-child who was
> born with an innate knowledge of himself and other peo-
> ple (& their *bodies*!) and the natural world. At times he's a
> brilliant fisherman, catching fish with flies and methods
> that seem utterly wrong. But he lacks the patience and ri-
> gor to be a truly great sportsman. Then again, I don't
> need another brilliant *fisherman* in my life.

McGarr dog-eared a corner of the page and closed the volume; diaries, he had always believed, were a bad idea, since they froze feelings that often changed as time went by. Then, of course, a diary might fall into somebody else's hands and spoil that person's appreciation of who you were or had been. If a person had to write down her thoughts, why not then burn them? Private thoughts were best left private.

He returned his attention to the photograph, noting details he had missed earlier. Stearns was wearing jeans and what appeared to be a tooled leather belt with a hammered silver buckle. The center was a massive turquoise stone, just the color of his eyes. He had a long, thin face that was shadowed by a Stetson, the band of which was bristling with bright salmon and trout flies. There was another knobby silver band on the wrist that was wrapped around Nellie's shoulder; it, too, was studded with smaller turquoise stones.

His thigh waders—McGarr recognized from fishing catalogs—were an older American style that would never do in Ireland. Made of some bleached canvas material, they were a buff color that might be suited to a western American river with a sandy bottom but would in Ireland scare trout. Or salmon. They looked well, however, with the Stetson hat and matching fishing vest, and, in all, he appeared as though he had stepped out of the pages of *Gentleman's Quarterly*, a magazine that McGarr's wife, Noreen, sometimes flicked through. "Where was this taken?"

"On the Moy."

McGarr glanced toward the mantel and his own portrait that had also been taken on the Moy. He shook his head, knowing he had no right to feel jealous. But yet he did. At least his own photo had pride of place. "Where was the fishing cowboy this afternoon?" he blurted out; he had seen nobody like Stearns at the wake.

"One of the locals told me he's been crazy drunk since Nellie's death. Ranting and raving. One of the neighbors called the Guards, who went out to calm him down."

"Out where?"

"To a cottage he's rented in Maghera."

McGarr tried to calm himself, but failed: the son of a bitch did not even have the generosity of spirit to think of Nellie or Nelson, only of himself and drowning his sorrow.

He stood. "Why, for Jesus' sake, would she ever think of entering the Owenea while it was in spate?"

Her father only shook his head and again looked toward the casket.

"Was her rod found?"

"No. Not yet."

Or not ever, if it was a Hardy. McGarr himself had only ever had one, given to him by Nellie, that he risked only when conditions were fair. He could not afford to replace it.

Or perhaps she had never had a rod with her. Could she have been *thrown* into the river? In turning her corpse over, McGarr noted the poorly stitched gash on her scalp, done obviously by the undertaker as a cosmetic patch. "Had Nellie any enemies?"

Nelson had to think. "I don't know if you'd call them enemies, but there were the drift-netters that she went up against."

McGarr knew what Millar meant by a drift net, having read about them in the papers. Nets of monofilament line, which most species of fish could not see, were being floated off the coast of the country, some of them stretching up to thirty miles in length. In them were caught everything—fish, birds, seals, dolphin, and whales, to say nothing of salmon. Only preferred species were kept. The rest were discarded as "trash" fish. Dead.

As few as ten years ago, only forty percent of the salmon taken in Ireland were caught by nets of all types. At that time fifteen percent were taken by rod and reel. Now over eighty percent were snagged by drift nets alone, and angling's share had declined to four percent. Rod fishers, of course, had been complaining, and he could imagine that Nellie had joined that fight.

"They're a rough lot. But it's nothing that anybody who was...right would kill over."

But there were many who weren't *right* in any way, McGarr knew all too well. He had seen people murdered over an insult, the phase of the moon, or the price of a pint. Or a fix. "Are there any waders in the house that would fit me?"

Nelson squinted down at McGarr's shoes. "Probably a size large."

"Wading staff, rod, jacket, hat?"

Understanding why McGarr was asking, the older man nodded. "Of course."

"You'll lose the waders."

"I have other pairs. Shall I come with you? It might still be dangerous," to wade in, he meant.

"I'd like that, but"—He glanced toward Nellie.

"Sure, I'll get somebody in. We won't be gone for long, and—to tell you the truth—I need a break."

# 4

# Reenactment

In part as an experiment to learn how Nellie Millar had died, but also as an elegiac act, Peter McGarr arrived on the banks of the Owenea River, a mile from Ardara, at dusk that night. Nelson Millar was with him.

The sky to the west was lit as with pale pink fire, when suddenly the sun appeared below the line of clouds out in the Atlantic. Watching it sink, McGarr waited for that exquisite moment when it was finally quenched and emitted its brilliant, emerald-green glint—tonight a spark in every way!—that Nellie had first pointed out to him. It was something in the natural world that he had not seen before, and she had shown him.

Fishing for her had been much more than the act of catching fish. It had been the birds, the trees, the natural life both in and out of the streams, rivers, and lakes she had fished. Clouds.

McGarr glanced up at a cloud bank so towering and

distant that it was still catching the direct rays of the now vanished sun. There its mountains and valleys—brilliant against a blue-black sky—were slowly muting in the ether. Farther to the east in the darkness, the sky was a welter of bright stars. McGarr hoped that the spirit which was Nellie was now somewhere among them, or in the depths of her beloved Owenea, which from the car park by the bridge he now could hear roaring.

With genuine anger to think—and he was still not convinced—that somebody might have..."worked" her demise and that she had actually died, he unclasped the largest blade of his pocketknife. It was very sharp, but the point was not stout enough to breach the composite material so that the blade could slice the required four inches.

Nelson had to show him where the filleting knife was located in the fishing jacket McGarr was wearing. Yet even with its six-inch blade, he had to punch and pull the knife to vent the material. But unlike the attempt with the fragment of broken glass, the breach was fair and a near match with the cut in the waders Nellie had been wearing when she died.

The two men then crossed the road and climbed the stile in the wall of the bridge, walking along the verge of a meadow toward the only pool Nelson knew of that might require wading to cast across. Twice by the light of the nearly full moon he saw the phosphorescent flash of a salmon break the surface of the water, one of a size that made him blink and want to throw out a fly.

McGarr always preferred a ripple on the water when fishing for salmon, and now, as night came on, a favorable west wind, counter to the flow of the river, sprang up. When they got to the pool, however, they found that the steep hill made it difficult to cast, both because of surrounding vegetation and the fact that the hillside created a basin that caused the wind to swirl.

To reach the pool near the farther bank where he had caught salmon in the past and, Nelson said, where the big fish would be lying, McGarr either had to walk the three quarters of a mile back to the bridge and another again up to the pool, or he had to enter the water here. Not even a well-executed Spey cast (a maneuver that did not require back-casting) would place the fly where it was needed. From the farther bank, however, he would be silhouetted against the moon and visible to the salmon. They discussed it, and agreed that here must be the spot that Nellie had begun to wade.

It was difficult in the dark, seeing where to place his feet. Even testing the depths did not help much, since the small round rocks that formed the bottom pushed away under the end of the wading staff. His feet slid down them, and the current caught his body. He was swirled in a circle—one hand on the fly rod; the other on the staff— until he managed to wedge the staff between two large boulders and gain his feet.

He was up to his ribs in the river now, and he could feel the trickle of cold water down the small of his back into the boots of the waders. The thunder of the river was now deafening and distracting. As he began the pendulum movement of casting, the rocks beneath his feet shifted, and the current tugged at him. Some flotsam—a branch or a log; it was by him before he could see what it was— struck him in the chest.

And yet with the wading staff pressed firmly against his hip, he managed to place the fly somewhere within the pool proper. But what would he do if he actually hooked a salmon of size? There would be no question of moving anything but the rod, and even that action would be restricted.

Now both legs of the waders were filled to the knees. Quickly he reeled in the line and waited no more than a minute or two, until he felt the last bit of air bubble around his waist. He then turned and tried to make his way back to the bank where Nelson Millar was waiting.

With a slight tug he freed the wading staff from the crevice in the boulders, and it shot out of his hands downstream, flailing in the torrent on its leather thong. He had difficulty snatching it back. Pushing off against a boulder, he then tried to spin toward the shore, but his legs were leaden, and the stones slid from under his feet, like marbles in a bin.

Lunging, he handed the rod up to Nelson, then he used the staff like a paddle in the rocks to propel himself into the lee of the bank. Waving off the older man's proffered hand, he managed to heave his torso up onto the bank and worm his way out of the water.

But McGarr was a well-muscled thirteen-and-a-half-stone man. His legs were powerful, and without a surfeit of upper-body strength, he would not have been able to accomplish the maneuver.

Said the older man, "Why did she *ever* think of going into this river? It must have been even more savage, the night—" He could not go on; he glanced up at the moon.

It was *the* question, of course. To catch salmon? Or a big salmon? Or perhaps she had hooked a salmon, and the line had gotten snagged, and— There was no way of knowing. McGarr had to ask himself what he *did* know:

That Nellie *might* have been murdered by somebody who knew she would fish the river at night in spate and most probably alone. What would that require?

Access to the waders sometime shortly before she put them on—where? Most probably in the car park where

McGarr himself had donned the pair he was wearing. One did not dress for fishing before reaching a stream: waders were awkward to walk in and the bottoms of the boots—felt, rubber grip, or (as in this case) metal studs—could be worn down on concrete or tar. As well, one did not drive with waders, which were wide and could result in pedal confusion. "Nellie arrived here in her own car?"

Millar nodded. "It was found here the next morning."

"Locked?"

"I don't know. The Guard—Sergeant Treacy—said he'd collect it for me, if I wished, and I gave him the key."

"Because it was locked?"

Millar straightened up. "Now that you mention it, he said it was."

"I know I asked you before, but can you think of any reason anybody would have wanted . . . this to happen to Nellie?"

Nelson shook his head. "And don't think I haven't been asking myself. Everybody *loved* Nellie, you know that yourself." But not well enough, went unsaid.

For the first time that day—in fact, for the first time in *any* day—McGarr realized he had not thought of his own wife and child, who would have been waiting to hear from him. Which only added to the curious, almost schizophrenic guilt he was feeling. To have abandoned Nellie, only to have something like this happen to her. And now to have abandoned Noreen and Maddie, if only in his thoughts.

"When in Ireland," he remembered a police friend and mentor once telling him, "think guilt. Guilt rules all."

He removed the waders, poured the river water from the legs, and flopped them over his shoulders. Together with Nelson Millar, he turned back toward the car park.

Every so often the moon, appearing from between racing

53

clouds, bathed the newly mown field beside the river in a timeless, achromatic light. Hayricks became chalk dolmens and still-pasturing sheep in a farther field white, slowly moving plinths. Often with Nellie, McGarr had slept out in fields like this—no, in this very field as well—in order to fish the dawn.

For her, for him, for *them* (he now promised her), he would discover what had happened to her and by whom.

"What was that, a reenactment?" a man's voice asked as they approached the bridge, which was in deep shadow.

McGarr stopped and waited; whoever it was, he had something to tell them.

"At least you've got the time right."

McGarr checked the luminous dial of his watch. It was half twelve. "How do you know?"

But there was no answer, and by the time they climbed the stile and reached the road, he was gone. They heard a motor start in the car park—two cylinders, a "Deux Chevaux"?; yes, an old, battered van—which then rattled up the road north toward Narin and Maas.

At the Garda barracks in Ardara, where McGarr repaired to check Nelson's report of the break-in, Sergeant Treacy told him that the only "Deux Chevaux" he knew of in the area was owned by one Hal Shevlin. "A poacher of note. Draft-netter. *Drift*-netter—the one the government ran in two or three months ago for fishing too close to the mouth of the bay. Maybe you read about it. They took his boat, his nets. The lot. A hard man, and a bitter man, I'd say."

Nelson and McGarr exchanged glances. "Where does he live?"

"Out in Rossbeg. On the right when you get to the beach. The low house by the jetty."

"May I use your phone?"

"If it's official. And, if it is, I'd like to know why. Don't mind my asking, but aren't you still under the . . . suspension, Chief Superintendent?"

"Can you keep a secret?" McGarr asked, picking up the receiver.

"Of course."

"Then listen and hold your tongue."

The first call was to Detective Superintendent Hugh Ward, who was McGarr's temporary replacement as head of the Serious Crimes Unit; the second was to his wife, Noreen, whom he roused from her sleep.

"This is more complicated than I first thought, I'm afraid, and the weather seems to be holding." Donegal was beautiful and its beaches were unequaled, but the weather here could be erratic, even in high summer. "Maybe you and Maddie would like to join me. I'll make the arrangements at this end." He could not—and *would* not—reveal the real reason that he wanted them near, which was a prime piece of selfishness, he was certain.

"Sure. Great. We could do with a bit of a holiday. But . . . more complicated *how*?" Noreen, he sometimes thought, enjoyed what he was—or, at least, had been—in his professional life more than who he was himself. And she compelled him to discuss with her any case that she found interesting; often he had found her counsel helpful.

In this instance, however, it was McGarr who needed her. The truth was that McGarr was feeling . . . lost or detached or, at least, in some way strange suddenly to find himself back in a former life. And the feeling would be less, he imagined, if Noreen and Maddie were present to remind him of the choice he had made those many years before.

"Are you saying that your Nellie was—"

"I'll say when you get here."

"Ah, Peter. Just a bit of it. Something to ponder on the road."

"When you get here. And drive slow."

# PART II

Angling is casting into the back chambers of
our minds.

—COTTON MATHER

# 5

# The Better Part
# of Valor

Unlike Noreen McGarr, Detective Superintendent Hugh Ward was not yet asleep at 1:10 A.M. When his electronic beeper sounded—announcing McGarr's call—he could not have been in a setting more different from the dayroom of a Garda barracks in distant Donegal. He was ensconced in the plush of deep banquette in Lillie's Bordello, a trendy after-hours club down an alley off Dublin's stylish Grafton Street.

Beside him was a dark, willowy young woman who was dressed in a scanty red silk dress. The sheen on her legs was such that it appeared as though she were wearing the sheerest of stockings; actually it was her skin, which had the color and gloss of buff, polished marble. Ward could not keep himself from imagining how that cool-looking skin would feel, say, against his cheek.

Every so often the toe of a flat black dancing slipper—a shapely pinion swinging on crossed knees—nicked the cuff of his trousers. Ward glanced away, trying to look unmoved. It was counterproductive, he had long ago discovered, to show too much interest, once the ice, so to speak, had been broken.

Ward had met the young woman, who could not be any more than twenty-one, only a hour or so past, after putting in a long day in the Dublin Castle headquarters of the Serious Crimes Unit, which he now commanded. He could not face the prospect of returning to his meticulously considered, bachelor digs alone. "Pad," while accurate, was a term that Ward eschewed.

Ward had trouble sleeping of late, and he understood what he needed to rectify the situation—a long, exhausting bout of uninhibited, cathartic sex, which he had not experienced in more time than he cared to remember. By choice, which was hard to believe, knowing himself as he did. All too well.

At thirty-two, Hughie Ward was a small, dapper man with dark good looks and a well-exercised, classically formed body that had led him to two European amateur boxing championships in the seventy-kilo-weight class. In amorous combat, however, Ward had performed yet more stirringly (he had been told), and there was a time in his life when he had sparred with as many combatants of the opposite sex as his stamina and the demands of his profession would allow. Only once did he find a partner equal to his needs and able to sustain his interest, which was his present problem, since she had made herself unavailable to him. For good, he feared.

Not actually expecting much of Lillie's Bordello, Ward had told the bouncer at the door, who knew him from the ring, that his visit was not official, and he was only interested in having a "scoop or two" before going home. But he had no sooner obtained a pint and turned away from the bar to find a quiet nook, then he saw her. The lady in red.

She had just entered the "Bordello," of all names, among a crowd of other, expensively dressed, near children. Or, rather, ahead of them, walking with a quick, fluid stride that made the most of her glorious legs and the flimsy red dress. Her purpose, he discovered, was to set her purse down at a vacant table, so she could rush out onto the parquet floor and dance to a sprightly rendition of "Walk on the Wild Side," which had just begun to play.

Why? Because she could *dance* on the wild side, Ward averred—with a graceful freneticism that revealed through the clinging silk the rest of her pleasingly coltish anatomy. Ward immediately fell in the sort of half-lust that had afflicted him recently.

He carried his pint over to her table and took a seat beside her purse. When after several other numbers, she finally returned, he stood, saying, "Sorry—I didn't realize the table was taken." In such a way, she could see all of his particulars; if not to her taste, he would hie himself off, as it were. There were too many good-looking women in the world to waste himself on somebody who was unappreciative. It was something Ward had been telling himself for nine months now.

"Nonsense," she replied. "You saw me the moment I walked in the room, the way I saw you. You saw me put down my purse. You watched me dance. You scarcely looked away once."

"I like the way you move." Speed being her number, he suspected.

"And how is that?" She allowed her eyes to sweep his features, his Armani suit and tie; they returned to his lips. Her pupils dilated. Briefly. Torridly.

"With graceful abandon. You *enjoy* dancing."

"You don't move so badly yourself. Can you dance too?" She had long jet-black hair and gray eyes. Prominent cheekbones and a thin, aquiline nose suggested some Spanish connection that Ward himself shared on his mother's side.

"I'd prefer to watch you. You don't really need a partner. For dancing."

"Sit," she said. "What are you having?"

It was a question fraught with possibility. Ward detested the process of having to "chat up" a woman for a decent period of time before suggesting they share a cool libation back at his flat on the quays, which he had retrofitted and furnished to a T that virtually sold him as tasteful, upwardly mobile, and assuredly (he would assure them) discreet. Therefore lovable. Or at least lustable, which was where he would draw the line from now on.

But then he noticed the barmaid by his elbow and realized that the lady in red only wished to buy him a drink. They sat, they drank, and he learned that she had recently graduated from Trinity (modern languages) and was about to continue her studies at the Sorbonne. Her parents, who were "troglodytes," were presently on holiday in Portugal, and she had decided to "live a little."

"What about your companions?" Ward inclined his head to the two large, possessive young men who had been glaring at them since they had begun to converse.

"Oh, they're just some *boys* I went to school with."

It was then that Ward's beeper went off.

"Are you a physician?" she asked as he removed the device from his belt and in the dim light squinted down at the number.

Ward recognized the area—Donegal—but not the number. Yet he would not have been contacted at this hour, by any one of the handful of people who had access to the beeper, were it not important. "I hope you'll think so, after we get to know each other. If you'll excuse me—I really should catch this call."

"You're coming back?"

"I couldn't keep myself away."

Leaving, he heard one of her friends say, "Know who he is?"

By the time he returned, she would probably know more (and better) about him than he knew himself—the police, the boxing, his recent promotion for having distinguished himself while on duty during the assassination crisis in Kerry, the fact that he was the youngest-ever head of the Murder Squad. It would save him from having to reveal those details modestly, self-denigratingly, later that morning. And if she was above dating a cop, so be it; passing by the bar, he saw a few other pairs of heavily mascaraed eyes follow him to the phone.

Most women found Ward "dangerous," which was how it was usually said. After all, he carried a gun and was known to have knocked many a bigger man on the flats of their backs. His ex-, as he now thought of former Detective Inspector Ruth Bresnahan, had called him "cuddly," since, as it turned out, it had been she who had been dangerous. For him.

"Chief?" he asked, when a familiar voice answered the Donegal number.

McGarr explained the circumstances of the death of Nellie Millar and added, "It's probably something I could handle alone at this end, if I weren't so well known. If people think I think it's murder, I'll get nowhere. The whole informer thing. And I could do with somebody who would be privy to local gossip."

"Well, I haven't yet taken my holidays, and I think I could see my way clear to—"

"No—you're too readily identifiable as well. And not country enough. You know who I was thinking of?"

Ward had no idea.

"Rut'ie," McGarr said in the flat, pancake accent that placed him as a Dubliner, born and bred.

The very woman, thought Ward.

"You know—a professional woman on holiday. She'd heard of Nellie Millar and always wanted to learn to fish the proper way. Now she's just staying on for the beach, don't you know. If later she's asked, she could say that she did not misrepresent herself. If it comes to court."

Ward's mind flooded with thoughts of how Ruthie looked in a bathing costume—worshipable—and how she swam—like a great, glorious dolphin, the waves just sliding off her back. In spite of his athleticism, Ward himself didn't swim a stroke, but he was a great man for admiring talent in others, especially those, such as she, who were tall, broad, well-formed, and touched something deep in him that he had been struggling to forget.

Also the possibility occurred to him of dropping up to Donegal to add "an official presence," the phrase even now came to mind, since McGarr was still under suspension and Ruthie no longer with the Garda. But he would have to learn more about her present state of . . . mind wasn't quite the word. Heart? He would not play the fool for her again.

"And yourself," he now said nonchalantly. "Have you heard from Ruthie recently?"

"I haven't, but Noreen bumped into her in Grafton Street the other day."

Ward straightened up and glanced toward the door as though Bresnahan might suddenly materialize there.

"Here in Dublin?" Gone was his coy tone. "When?"

"Last week."

"You're jokin'." And to think that she rang up nobody—
*him*—for, you know, old times sake or just to say how'rya.
Ward was suddenly deflated. He thought at least that they
would always be friends. Truly it was over, for her.

"Said she was up in town to buy some clothes, the shops
in Kerry not being up to her standard."

And where, pray tell, would she be wearing new clothes
in Kerry? he wondered. It was exactly what Ward had told
her when she delivered the devastating news that she was
resigning her position and returning to Sneem to manage
the farm of her father, who had died in the incident that
had injured Ward and made him so well known.

After seven years in Dublin, after *knowing him* and sharing a great (from his point of view) life together here where
things *happened*, she was no longer a Kerrywoman; she
was a Dub, like him. Hadn't he himself been born in pro-
vincial Waterford, where he would now not be caught
dead?

"They teamed up," McGarr went on, "and I got a grand
bill out of the afternoon. Hats, shoes, *suits!*"

And Noreen never let on to him. Ward himself had seen
Noreen recently in Dawson Street near her picture gallery.
Well—he glanced in the other direction toward the bar
and dance floor—he would now proceed to *bury* himself
in other women. Literally.

"Noreen said Rut'ie's having a tough go of it down
there."

Ward smiled; at least that was cheering.

"How did she put it, 'Nothing but cows, Culchies, tourists, and feckin' egomaniacs.' "

Ward knew to whom the last bit referred—one Rory
O'Suilleabhain (the King of Culchies [hicks!] in Ward's

book), who had been Ruthie's first love and who owned the adjoining farm. He was presently running for a seat in the Dail (the Irish parliament). "Is she living at home?"

"She told Noreen she was."

"What about his nibs?"

"O'Suilleabhain?"

Ward grunted; if he had the big feckin' farmer before him at that moment, he'd knock him in bits, so he would.

"I suspect he's at home. Noreen said Rut'ie only referred to him 'impersonally.' You know, never mentioned him by name, only said *he* and *your man*."

*Impersonally.* It sounded like a word that Noreen would use to say Ruthie was souring on the gobshite.

"Maybe Bernie would be better," McGarr went on, meaning Detective Superintendent Bernard McKeon, who was a skilled undercover man. "It's up to you. You're in charge."

Ward thought for a moment about how to say what he wished without revealing the depth of his desperation; he loved that big, flamboyant, uncaring, voluptuous, passionate, cold-hearted bitch from the bottom of his shallow, sexist, two-timing heart. "You know, if you really need her out there in Donegal, I see no problem in *you* asking her. Privately. Informally. I know for a fact that she can fish for salmon. Her father was the local Finn MacCool. Give her a buzz." He hoped the "*for me*" was not too naked in that. "And, of course, keep me informed," because I could be out there in a flash.

McGarr said, "I better think about it some more. I wouldn't want to disturb her."

Which was too damn indefinite for Ward.

"And one other thing. Could you run down one Henry 'Hank' Stearns for me? That's..." McGarr spelled the name. "He's an American, early thirties, and evidently he's been in this country for at least a year, so—."

"Immigration," Ward said.

"And anything we can get from the States, and not just a criminal record. Call in a favor, if you have to."

"Place of birth, military record, IRS—that class of thing?"

"You're well trained. I'll be at the Nesbitt Arms here in Ardara." McGarr rang off.

Stepping away from the phone, Ward felt like a yo-yo, tumbling after Ruth Bresnahan on the slightest hope she might again be his, and then—withdrawing wasn't the term at all—being snatched back to reality by the realization that she might have forgotten him altogether, as she probably had.

Walking through the ornate archway into the dancing lounge, Ward saw that the lady in red was still seated at the table, even though the music was wild, her eyes now on him. Her equally incarnadine lips parted in a patently libidinous smile. It was plain she did not mind cops. Or, rather, cop. An operative word.

Ward raised a finger, as though to say, Be back in another sec, and he moved in the direction of the gents' room.

Only to sneak out of the back door. Sullenly, sneakily, his tail most definitely between his legs.

# 6

# Rustic Diorama

After a short sleep back in his room at the Nesbitt Arms Hotel, McGarr climbed into his Cooper and headed out of town toward Maghera, where Hank Stearns, the "fishing cowboy," was reported to live.

The road traced a narrow path between Glengesh Hill—a promontory that rose over a thousand feet above the estuary of the Bracky River—and a steep strand. Donegal here was just as the last Ice Age had left it: a rounded, spectacular, treeless barren of towering mountains that plunged to the sand shores of the bay. Today the "hill" was enveloped in mist; out over the ocean a system of soft, textured clouds was racing, all blues and grays.

Perched on the flanks of the hill was the occasional shepherd's smallholding—a compound of tidy white cottage, a few outbuildings, a small pasture, and crumbling rock walls running straight up the precipitous slope to the top of the mountain. Seeing these last always made McGarr wonder who could have been moved to build them and why? And what they must have cost in toil and...life?

He knew—since Nellie had told him—that this part of
Donegal had been settled from earliest times, because
of the richness of the marine life in the bay. Remnants of
hunter-gatherer communities had been found in the sand
dating from 3000 B.C. At that time the interior of Ireland
had been nearly solid forest, and, possessing no means of
hewing timber, the Stone Age people had to content themselves with life in the dunes. Even after the advent of
metal tools, they returned here each summer for "shore
meat," as they called it: oysters, scallops, clams, mussels,
cockles, and sea trout and salmon that were taken by net
and spear.

He paused at a dramatic waterfall that was draining
some tannin-rich mountain lough. In blond cascades it fell
past grazing mountain sheep into a frothy pool that flowed
under the road toward the bay. A farmer on a bicycle with
a collie dog by his side stopped to pass the time of day,
and McGarr asked him where Stearns lived.

"Are yeh Irish?" the old man asked, eyeing his shirt and
tie and his gleaming older car.

McGarr nodded. "From Dublin."

"Then it's the bloody shieling on the side of the mountain
as you go up the valley of the Owenwee. You can't miss it."

Shieling. Again it was a term that McGarr had first heard
from Nellie, and referred to the mud and reed shelters that
had been constructed for milkmaids while boleying. Boleying was the old practice of pasturing sheep in mountain
commonages beginning on the twelfth of May (old May
Day) until the first sign of bad weather in September.
There the young women of nearby villages would watch
over the herds and flocks and also card and weave wool.

At night stories would be told—often by wandering poets
or men on the run—and on Sunday afternoon a singsong

and dance would take place in which a set piece was the recitation of a poem by the poet to the milkmaid of his choice. Obviously a pre-Christian tradition, it was discouraged by the Church and, beginning in the sixteenth century, outlawed by the British. Hence the rock walls running up the mountain?

McGarr craned his neck and glanced up again at the even greater imminence of Slieve Tooey, which he was fast approaching. Could the walls have had something to do with the breaking-up of the boolies? He would have to find out. Again, for Nellie.

Shieling was an exaggeration of the condition of Hank Stearns's house, but not by much. An ancient structure, it had been built in what, up until modern times, was the preferred position—perpendicular to the sharp slope of the mountain. In that way the family, who lived in the mountain end of the house, benefited from the insulation of the abutting earth, while the effluent of their animals, which lived in the other end, could be pushed out a door to flow down the hill.

Little apart from an absence of animals had changed in Stearns's cottage since those days. True, the dwelling no longer had a thatched roof; instead it was capped with corrugated metal, which would allow heat to escape, and was even rusted through in places. Nor could McGarr see electrical or telephone lines leading in. Paths were well beaten to a spring on the high side of the mountain and to an outhouse on the low.

A well-used Land Rover, its paint chipped and aluminum body dented, stood near the door. The yard was a sponge of peaty muck over which a few granite chips had been tossed years before. Stepping from one to another, McGarr approached the door, which opened when he was still a dozen yards away.

"If you're after Hank, he's not here," an American woman's voice said from the deep shadows within.

McGarr tried to peer into the darkness where, now, he could hear a baby crying and some other child saying, "Mommy—is it a bad man? Is it a bad man?"

"We'll see," the woman said, stepping out into the light but still within the house. She had an infant in one arm, but she kept the other hand behind her worn and spotted housedress, as though concealing something.

A gun was McGarr's first thought, and he glanced back at the Cooper. Contrary to the terms of his suspension, he still had a weapon under the seat, and there was something about the woman's manner that made him feel suddenly vulnerable.

She was tall, wide but gaunt. A blonde, her face was bony, which made her light-colored eyes look sunken. She had raised her head in a kind of challenge that McGarr had seen before and meant not one step farther. "I said, if you're looking for Hank, he's not here." There were flip-flops on her knobby feet, and another child—a towhead dressed in a stained jumper and bunched nappy—now appeared from the shadows and wrapped his arms around her thin legs. Still, McGarr could hear yet another child within the cottage, which made three at present count.

"Can you tell me where I can find him?"

In a gesture designed to put her at her ease, McGarr shook a cigarette from a packet, then offered it to her.

She only regarded him, the hand remaining behind her.

"Is he a bad man, Mommy?" the boy asked again, his childish accent also identifiably American.

"Who are you?"

"Peter McGarr's the name. I'm a friend of Nellie Millar, or at least—"

*Death on a Cold, Wild River*

"You're the cop Hank said would be coming." It was not a question.

McGarr waited, but when she said no more, he ventured, "You're American, aren't you, Mrs. Stearns?"

Still nothing.

McGarr remembered a packet of Smarties he had bought for Maddie some days earlier but had forgotten to give her. He now showed the sweets to the little fella, then squatted down and held out his hand, offering it to him. "Montana, like Hank?"

The child glanced up at his mother, seeking permission to take the sweets, but her bead on McGarr did not waver.

"Tell me, how do you find Ireland? Is it to your liking?"

"What's here to like? Henry said he was going to the caves down by the beach. Tell him I need money and the key to the car. Now!" She stepped back into the shadows, and the child glanced longingly at the sweets before following her inside without complaint. The door closed.

McGarr straightened up. Again looking around the boggy yard, he decided there was not much to like in the Ireland that was presented there. Apart from the view down the glen toward the bay, which was magnificent. But not readily edible.

The caves of Maghera lie at least a long mile from the nearest road. McGarr had to trudge along narrow paths that traced the ridges of grassy sand dunes. Sheep had preceded him, along with the shoeprints of a large man—size twelve at least, the toe cut square for riding. Drifting sand had obscured all but a few.

The wind was stronger still when McGarr dropped down onto the harder sand of the tide-stranded beach. There it was a staggering blast of windblown sand, which stippled his eyes and coated his tongue whenever he gasped for a breath; he had to turn his back and hurl himself at the tempest, and by the time he reached the protection of an outcropping, he could feel the sand trickling down the small of his back.

There the wind stopped with an abruptness that made his ears ring. He glanced up. The mouth of the first cave, which he could see, gaped at the top of a seventy-yard sand hill that lay at about a seventy-degree angle to the face of Slieve Tooey. It was a narrow ovoid of black basalt in the ginger-colored granite that was the headland of the mountain. What was left of the footprints in the sand that led up formed a sort of staircase to the top, McGarr imagined.

He was wrong. The sand gave way under his weight, and he had to take two or three steps to advance one. Straight up. When was the last time he had attempted something like this? Never, really. And there he was fully middle-aged—a smoker, a drinker, a lover of high-cholesterol foods, and a husband and father who was presently unemployed—risking myocardial infarction running down (or up) a reportedly drunken fishing cowboy from Montana in a sea cave in the West of Ireland. Let us pray.

By the time he reached the mouth of the cave, which was wide, he was panting. His brow was beaded with sweat, and he had to loosen his tie. Rewarding himself with another cigarette (and in such a way announcing his presence), he stepped into the darkness, which was very still and blessedly cool.

The cave was part of a system that dotted the base of Slieve Tooey every fifty yards or so. It had been formed, McGarr suspicioned, eons ago when pockets of soluble stone had been eroded by wave action from the base of the cliffs. Either the land had subsequently risen, or the ocean had receded. But this first cave was about fifty by fifty feet with a forty-foot reach to its highest point. And it was so perfectly maded that the gentle curves, rising equally from all sides to the arched ceiling, looked like corbeled black stone.

The floor was composed of the fine, powdery beach sand that bore the imprint of shoes and feet from dozens of visitors, since there was no breeze to disturb them. The smoke from McGarr's cigarette rose in a perfect lazy plume toward the apogee. But the cave was empty.

Turning to leave, McGarr was presented with a brilliant, sun-drenched diorama of Ireland: a white sand beach, turquoise water in the bay, the emerald swath of Loughros Point with its neat cottages and patterned fields. There waves were crashing into the cliffs, sending up plumes of diamond spray.

It was then somebody spoke, startling him, the voice echoing around the vaulted ceiling and sounding deep and orotund:

"In sixteen forty-two over five hundred men, women, and children entered this cave to escape Cromwell's army, which was ravaging Donegal and was headed this way. An informer revealed their whereabouts. Only one man escaped the massacre. He scrambled up here onto this shelf and witnessed the murder of his family, friends, and neighbors. He lived to be a very old man.

"Question—how did he go on? Did he in any way feel guilty, you know, to have lived when everybody else that he knew died? Did he bury at least his own family or, say, attempt to seal the mouth of the cave? As a tomb? Maybe that's why there's so much fine sand here.

"One day a few months ago I got out a shovel and came up here and began digging. It took me all day to find this."

A disk of something fell into the sand by McGarr's feet. Squatting down, he picked it up. It was an irregularly formed gold sovereign with James I's head on one side, the Stuart crest on the other. The date 1609 was barely legible.

"I wonder how it was missed, but with all that carnage . . ."

McGarr looked back out at the sunny diorama. "Nellie tell you that—about the massacre?" It was something she would have known about Ardara.

"And other things." For instance, about you, went unsaid.

"Your coin." McGarr held the sovereign, as though he would scale it back up to Stearns.

"I don't want it now."

"Of course you do." It had to be worth a fair amount of money. When Stearns said nothing, McGarr slipped it into a coat pocket; he would give it to Stearns's . . . woman, or whatever she was to him, back at the cottage. She would find some use for it, he was sure.

"You're the man from the mantel." Obviously he meant the mantel in Nellie's sitting room. "The one from the 'g-yards,' " he added in a broad Midlands brogue.

"Formerly of the g-yards. Currently I'm a citizen."

"That's right—the assassination thing." Stearns's dismissive tone, to say nothing of his nasally American accent, set McGarr's teeth on edge. The "assassination thing" included not only the death of a much-respected Taosieach, but also one of his ministers and eight other people, including Ruth Bresnahan's father. Hugh Ward had been injured and could have been killed. McGarr's own career was now under a cloud that might well result in permanent suspension.

"Nellie followed it in the papers and on TV," Stearns went on. "Even canceled a week of our classes, she was so concerned."

*Our* classes? "And which classes would they have been?" McGarr asked, struggling to keep his own voice even and his eyes on the diorama presented in the cave mouth.

"Fly-fishing classes—didn't her father tell you about me?"

That he had, thought McGarr. "You mean, you assisted Nellie when she taught her fly-fishing classes?" McGarr couldn't keep himself from glancing up at the man.

Stearns had something before his face that looked like a bottle; he pulled it down. "We were more like partners, actually. Most of the women are a bit long in the tooth. Have to be to pay the freight. At the end there, Nellie was getting a thou a week apiece, to say nothing of the tackle and books and videos she sold them. Some of her 'graduates' would trade with nobody else at—get this!—eighteen-fifty a pop for a salmon fly tied personally by Nellie Millar, but mostly with substitute feathers. Pounds, I'm talkin', not dollars."

By substitute feathers Stearns meant those taken from common or domesticated birds and not from exotic or endangered species.

"You know, well-heeled divorcées or spinsters or the old cows who're getting into fly-fishing so they can offer Daddy a little companionship now that they're over the hill. Nellie said I added another dimension."

"Really?" It was a change from what Nellie had told McGarr she wished to establish, when first coming to Ardara—a place where a woman could come and learn to fish without feeling any pressure or having the distraction of men about. "You know—to learn something disinterested that a woman might grow to love by herself. And *for* herself," was how she had put it. McGarr now asked, "And how exactly did you help Nellie?"

"In *every* way," Stearns blurted out, his tone now nearly gloating. "You know, Nellie had a heck of a reputation, and much of it was deserved. In the quiet water of a chalk stream or a lake—hey, there was nobody who could present a midge or an ephemeral better. She was one of the first women to fish professionally, and she sure could write." But she was a woman, was the implication. "You drink?"

McGarr's gorge was now so high that he could barely bring himself to shake his head. It was a complex of emotions—distaste, jealousy, anger, outrage—that he knew he had no right to be feeling. But if it turned out that this wretch on the shelf had been the one who had "worked" Nellie's death, he did not know what he would do, but it would not be pretty.

He could not keep his eyes from darting up at Stearns, who was reclining comfortably on the ledge, his head against the back wall of the cave so that the buff cowboy hat nearly covered his eyes. The brim had been curled and the crown shaped to look "authentic," McGarr judged.

Beneath it, Stearns's eyes were the color of the turquoise stone in his hammered silver belt buckle, and the curl of his upper lip repeated the retroussé curve of his long, thin nose. The blonding shoebrush moustache was precisely clipped. The boots below his cuffless Levi's were black with silver toe caps and more silver detailing on the sides. Stearns reached a liter bottle out into the light of the cave mouth. Wild Turkey, a kind of bourbon that in Ireland was nearly impossible to find and cost at least double the price of whiskey. It was nearly finished.

Again McGarr thought of the gaunt woman and the children back in the rude cottage. He ignored the bottle. "My question was, how *exactly* did you help with the classes?"

"Oh—mainly I was there. I mugged a lot." Stearns showed McGarr his white, even teeth. "Did demonstrations with the equipment while Nellie talked. Streamside, I'd help the gals who were having trouble getting the beat." He gestured with his hands to mean the rhythm of casting a fly. "A smile here, a touch there, an encouraging word."

"And you liked that?"

Stearns shrugged. "All in a day's work."

"And the women. The women were the thing."

"Always have been. Always will be. How 'bout yourself? I understand you got a young wife."

"Like you."

"Jane's not my wife, and Jane's never been young. Not ever. She was *born* with the mentality of a forty-year-old."

McGarr loathed people who disparaged their own, especially to a complete stranger. The man might be drunk, but his statement said as much about him as about the woman Jane.

"And your children? How many of them are there anyhow?"

Stearns shrugged and looked down at the bottle, which was now empty. "Every man should have children."

And care for them.

"So—what brings you here?" Stearns asked, sitting up on the shelf so that his booted feet hung over the edge. "You want to compare notes about Nellie, or just shoot the breeze?"

McGarr only eyed him.

"You knew her about ten years ago, didn't you? Ten years can mean a lot in a woman. But then I guess she was about your age, wasn't she?"

McGarr sprang out of his squat, seized Stearns by his cowboy jacket, and dragged him down off the ledge, throwing him into the sand. "Move, you feckin' bollocks, and I'll kick you senseless."

The hat was off Stearns's head, and his arms were thrown back; his eyes were glassy, as with fright, but clear. If he had drunk all that bourbon, McGarr would eat the bottle.

"Tell me about the night Nellie died. Was it you she went out to the Owenea with?"

Stearns nodded.

"Who drove?"

"I did."

"Whose car?"

"Mine."

"Your what?"

"Rover."

"What time?"

"Dusk."

"Did you fish together?"

"No—I wanted to, but she said it was something she had to do herself."

McGarr waited.

"Catch a trophy fish, she had been saying for days. Maybe a week. Ever since *Eire Rod & Reel* came out. There was a letter to the editor in it about how she had never proven herself on a spate river, not even the Owenea. It was bothering her. She told me to go fish on my own, that she wasn't returning to Ardara until she had one. So I decided to walk up the river and fish down.

"But when I got back to the Rover, her things were gone, and I figured I either missed her in the dark, or she passed me while I was playing a fish. Or she decided to nap and fish the dawn. There's a field there that just got hayed, and the ricks—"

McGarr nodded. The ricks were a good place to sleep, and he did not wish to hear Stearns brag that he too had slept in them with Nellie.

"But dawn was just breaking when I got back into town. And then I was surprised to see a light on in her shop when I drove by. I stopped and got out to ask her if she'd had any luck, since I got two good fish myself. She was sitting

80

at her tying table at the back of the shop, working over the vise. The door was locked. I knocked, but she waved me off. I figured she hadn't had any luck, but thought she knew a fly that would work, and she was dressing some."

"What did you use?"

"A Lemon and Gray. Size six."

It seemed odd to McGarr that Nellie had returned to the shop when salmon were taking Lemon and Grays. She would have had Lemon and Grays in all sizes with her. It was one of the premier flies for the Owenea, especially at night in spate conditions. "What did you do then?"

"I rapped on the door of the pub across the street."

"Nancy's," McGarr said. It was a pub that he himself had frequented.

"They let me in. I sold them the fish, had a pint, and went to bed."

McGarr thought for a moment. "How would Nellie have gotten into Ardara from the Owenea?"

Stearns shook his head. "She could have walked, but—"

But not in her waders. She would have taken them off and *carried* them into town along with her other gear? No, she would have stowed her gear in Stearns's Rover, if she thought he would fish through the night as well. And if she had planned to return to the river. "You mean, you didn't find her gear and tackle in your truck?"

Another head shake. "It's why I was surprised to see her back in the shop."

"What was she wearing at the tying table?"

"She had her back to the window. Fishing hat, I remember. Jacket, I guess. I don't know. Why do you ask?"

"Waders?"

"I didn't think to look. Like I said, she was sitting down, back to the window. It's a small place. Even the window is small and filled with tackle and stuff. I didn't think to look." Stearns's odd-colored eyes moved toward the brilliant mouth of the cave. "But if her gear wasn't in my truck, then she must have had them with her. Maybe she got a lift into town. If any local saw her walking at that time of night, they'd stop, especially with her loaded down with stuff.

"I don't know if this is news to you, or if you want to know, being a cop and all. But some of the pubs in the West here stay open most of the night in summer. There were still people on the streets. Somebody else must have seen her—on the road, in the shop."

There Stearns was on the flat of his back telling McGarr about Ireland. McGarr wondered what Nellie had seen in the man, but then he knew, didn't he?

"Can I ask you again, why the questions?"

"Where would your gear be—what were you wearing that night?"

"In the Rover."

"*All* of it?"

"I haven't fished since. Of course."

"Give me the key."

From the watch pocket of his Levi's, Stearns withdrew a single key and flipped it to McGarr.

"Now your wallet."

Stearns threw him that too.

McGarr was surprised to find three hundred British pounds in crisp fifty-pound bank notes. "The publican pay you with these? For the salmon?"

Yet again Stearns shook his head, his eyes on the wallet. "He paid me in Irish currency. I used that to buy the Turkey." He meant the Wild Turkey. "The following afternoon, when I heard about Nellie. I haven't had a chance to go to a bank," and exchange the British money that was somewhat more valuable than the Irish equivalent, he meant.

"Where'd you get this?" McGarr waved the British currency.

When Stearns said nothing, McGarr scaled the wallet back at him. With two of the fifty-pound notes.

"What's this, a stickup?"

"No—it's your contribution to your nonwife and family. And I'll tell you this—if any part of your story doesn't check out, I'll be back."

"Why—what's up?" Stearns shouted from the mouth of the cave as McGarr made his way down the steep, sandy slope. "What are you saying, that Nellie was murdered?"

McGarr was not saying it yet, but he would, when he had the murderer. And he was hoping it was Stearns.

Back at the cottage, he went straight for the Rover and slowly, methodically went through Stearns's fishing gear, tackle, jacket, and fly boxes. Most was of middling quality with the odd piece—from Nellie, he did not doubt—of the best. He found a variety of line snippers, tackle scissors, pliers, and tweezers but not one knife, which was unusual.

By the time he finished, Stearns was standing beside the vehicle. "I want to know why you're doing this. If I don't get an answer, I'm going to the Guards. As I remember, you're in enough trouble already."

"You always sell your fish to Nancy's?" McGarr asked, closing the door of the Rover.

"Among other pubs and restaurants."

"Clean them first?"

"Never—it's always easier to sell a whole fish. They look better, and who likes to gut?"

"Ever keep any yourself?" McGarr glanced at the door of the cottage, which had just opened.

"I never eat fish, and I . . . *we* need the money."

"So I gathered." McGarr moved toward the woman and children, who had appeared again in the doorway. He showed her the key and the money. "Did this man sleep here on the night Nellie Millar died?"

The woman, Jane by name, turned to Stearns and regarded him with undisguised contempt. "Which night would that be?"

"Three nights ago."

Again there was a pause while she and Stearns continued to make eye contact. "I can't remember."

"Why not?"

She hunched her wide, thin shoulders, looking for all the world like a Dorothea Lange portrait from the Great Depression. "It's not something that I would. He comes and goes as he pleases."

"Did you know that he was having an affair with Nellie Millar?"

Again she shrugged. "I guess it's over, isn't it? Now, are you going to give me that money?"

McGarr handed it to the little boy, along with the key, the gold coin, and the packet of Smarties.

Back at the Nesbitt Arms Hotel, a fax from Hugh Ward was awaiting him. It said Henry Luke Stearns had no prior criminal record. He had been born and raised in Niles, Ohio, a son of two assembly-line workers at the General Motors plant in nearby Lordstown. He had studied at Kent State University, also in Ohio, taking a Ph.D. in stream entomology. After teaching there for seven years, he was denied tenure, and he left.

On an IRS tax form three years ago, he filed jointly with a woman, Jane Trowbridge, who was listed as his wife. They claimed two dependent children, age two and three months respectively.

In the next year he claimed no income and listed his occupation as writer/lecturer. Last year, he did not file a tax claim and had no current U.S. address.

"I hope there's nothing wrong, Chief Superintendent?" the man behind the hotel desk asked. Obviously he had read the fax message and knew all too well who Henry Luke Stearns was and had been to Nellie Millar.

Again McGarr was reminded of the strictures of conducting—what was it? An investigation that could not be an official investigation, because of his suspension—in a small town in the West of Ireland. And even if it were official, he would go public only when forced to. Nobody in a place like this would . . . inform on anybody else. The families were large and extended and would hold a grudge, no matter the crime. Nellie might have been admired and even loved, but she had been, after all, a blow-in. From Mayo.

And there was the matter of when, exactly, Nellie had died: before dawn, as said by the man—Hal Shevlin, the former drift-netter, whom Nelson and he had met on the bridge? Or after, as Stearns had said? When had her waders been slit: before she went fishing with Stearns (and had not entered the stream) or after, when she returned alone? Had somebody else seen her in her shop with or without her waders, or brought her into town, obviously with the waders since Stearns had not found her gear in his Rover?

And a motive for her death. Who would have stood to gain? Certainly not Stearns, who would now be without any means of support beyond what he could pull from the Owenea before September 1, when the salmon season closed. Would Nellie have paid him in British sterling? Why, unless some one of her clients had paid her in sterling and then she paid him. . . .

"Nothing of the kind," McGarr said, smiling to the desk clerk. "I was just interested in who is who. Force of habit, I guess."

"Ah, yes—still in the traces," the man said affably. "The police work. Tell me, how's it all going in Dublin? The suspension and so forth."

McGarr then imparted a kernel of information about the proceedings of the Tribunal of Enquiry that had not made the papers. It would doubtless spark conversation wherever it traveled. Which would be to ALL PARTS, he was sure. In some ways a small town possessed advantages that Dublin could never hope to duplicate.

He then made arrangements for Noreen and Maddie, who would be arriving soon, and he moved his belongings to a new suite of rooms that was equipped with a telephone.

There he decided he should call Ruth Bresnahan down in Kerry, to see if she could lend the investigation ... not necessarily a hand. Rut'ie's hands, while large and nicely formed, were not necessarily the best part of her. McGarr was thinking of Henry "Hank" Luke Stearns, for whom women were the thing.

His second call was to Nelson Millar, asking him if he could come by for the keys to Nellie's shop.

# 7

# The Value of a Kind, Conciliatory Word

Former Garda Detective Inspector Ruth Bresnahan felt like she was in a time warp when the phone call from Peter McGarr reached her in her native Kerry shortly before noon. With roles reversed.

There she was standing at the kitchen sink in the house of her mother's three-hundred-acre farm outside Sneem. Her arms were plunged to the elbows in washing-up suds, and her mother was prattling from the den off the kitchen that had formerly been the nursery when Ruth was a baby, twenty-eight years ago.

Outside the window Rory O'Suilleabhain was stripped to his wondrously narrow waist, wrestling a large boulder that her father, who had also been a large man, had never had the strength to move.

In the strong sun of a midsummer day, sweat glistened on the powerful lines of O'Suilleabhain's body as he forced the lever down and the large boulder tumbled neatly, like so much papier-mâché, onto the fork of some one of his

many "mash-eens." He—"The O'Suilleabhain," as his
mother, God rest her soul, had referred to her only son in
her time—owned the neighboring farm. It was the only
one in the entire South Kerry Mountains that was better
than her own, and throughout her adolescence Ruth had
doted on Rory O'Suilleabhain, who was a few years older
than she, mostly from afar.

Any moment now, he would come into the house and
demand to know when they were going to set The Date
for their marriage. Rory had not done anything for her or
for her farm in the past month without asking her—gently
at first—that same question. Now he was at the end of his
tether. If she said yes, what would it mean? Nothing less
than committing herself for the rest of her life, she knew—
until she too was an old, dotty woman, like her mother.

True, Rory was standing for the Dail and would undoubtedly win the seat and go to Dublin. But she, as op-
posed to he, knew the city and its ways. And those of the
men who controlled government there. Rory O'Suilleabhain, in spite of his good mind, good looks, and un-
doubted country charm, would not be able to stick it for
very long. There was a certain, necessary denial of ego as
a backbencher that Rory would not be able to summon.
He was nothing if not himself. Always.

And after nine months, she knew she could not spend
the rest of her life here in Sneem, having *conquered* Dublin
in her own modest way. She might again, as Rory's wife,
but he would resent any success—even social—that might
eclipse his own. If she were to be his wife, it would have
to be on traditional terms, those that had wasted her
mother and had now given rise to the incessant chat from
the next room.

"You'll see, when you have your babbies, what a help it
will be to have these old bones about the place. Granted,

I only had yourself, but you were a handful and..." Her voice wound on.

The tractor out in the yard now started up, and O'Suilleabhain's sea-green eyes met Ruth's when the boulder swung round, as much as to say, I'm not slaving over this place for nothing. I'll be in to settle the thing and keep tongues from wagging. Together their joined farms would form an "agri-business," a term her recently deceased father once read in a newspaper and wrote down and pondered for days.

Which did not in any way obscure the fact that O'Suilleabhain had been a bounder. He had by-blows scattered over three counties, it was said. If he truly wanted her love, he would have to work for it, and not just with sweat.

It was then that the telephone rang. Her mother, who had picked up the receiver, appeared at the sink, saying, "It's for you. A man. He asked for Rut'ie. A Dub by the sound of him. The 'fella'?" she asked, meaning Hugh Ward, Ruth's former lover.

No, Ward was a young man, who had learned—as a matter of refinement—to pronounce his *h*'s. Ward had and would continue to get on in Dublin.

"Chief?" Ruth asked when she picked up the receiver.

"How did you know it was me?"

"Sure, who else would be calling me from Dublin?"

"Actually, I'm in Donegal. I'm wondering how busy you are and if you'd be available..." McGarr then explained what he thought he might need of her.

A break, she thought, as O'Suilleabhain entered the kitchen, where he moved to the tap and began sluicing his head, neck, and torso with cold water. Some time away so she wouldn't be blinded by his presence.

He was a magnificent physical specimen—six feet five

inches tall with two feet of shoulder to either side and a waist that was nearly as small as her own. The rest of him was as classically formed, but the problem was he knew it, and also knew that it was enough for most women. But not for her.

"Can I think about it?" she now said to McGarr. "Can I call you back tomorrow?"

"Of course, Rut'ie. The last thing I want to do is to put you out. If for any reason you think you can't, don't. I could as easily ask Hughie for Bernie, and he'll send him, he will." McGarr meant Detective Superintendent Bernard McKeon.

Bresnahan turned her back to O'Suilleabhain and stepped into the den, where her mother was busy listening to her every word. "Have you heard from him?" She meant Ward.

Her mother began tsking; she shook her head.

"Yah," said McGarr.

"How is he?"

"Busy. He's shorthanded as it is, and now there's the holidays."

Has he been asking after me? she nearly asked, but only said, "He'll get by, I'm sure. What about yourself?" meaning the Tribunal of Enquiry.

"Solicitors, judges, and politicians—it's out of me hands. You'll phone tomorrow?" McGarr gave her the number and rang off.

"Who was that?" O'Suilleabhain asked, while drying himself in the middle of the kitchen.

Ruth only smiled wanly and returned the receiver to its yoke, hating herself for her coyness. There, she wasn't even married to the man, and already she was playing games—which would be necessary, she knew—to keep him from subsuming her, body and soul.

His brow glowered and his nostrils dilated, sure signs that he was becoming angry. His fists even came up on his hips. "Look—I want an answer. When will it be, the date? You're making a laughingstock of me in the village."

Ruth had heard through a friend what was being said: "He'll be as long engaged to her, as he was courting the county." She now returned to the dishes in the sink, saying, "I told you—when I finish mourning my father."

"Sure, your father wanted nothing better for you himself," her mother said from the den, taking O'Suilleabhain's side. After all, being a farmer's wife was all she had known herself.

"*And* when I'm certain it's what I choose to do. You wouldn't want me otherwise."

It was an argument that always made the best of damnable good sense to O'Suilleabhain, who, she imagined, had said as much to many an otherwise good young woman in his time. "Well, tonight then—will you be coming out?" He meant down to the pub so, at closing time, she could be seen leaving with him. Whatever did or did not happen between them could be left up to "shpeck-oo-lay-tion," as was said, and his reputation for swordsmanship would be left somewhat intact.

Ruth glanced out the window at the pit that had been left by the removal of the rock. Why not? Things could change even after the longest time. It would be the test of how he could deal with his ego, to say nothing of her. And of how she felt about him and them together there in Sneem. For life. She had been putting him off far too long and cruelly so, getting back at him for all those years when they had been young and she had pined after him. And he had snubbed her.

By nightfall it was still hot, and Ruth decided to give the man the kind of show that he most wanted his friends to see. As when stepping out with her women friends in Dublin of an evening, she applied "war paint," then selected the most provocative "country" costume that she could piece together from her profoundly urban wardrobe.

It combined a jeans-styled stretch miniskirt in tangerine, which was just the color of her hair. And a white, off-the-shoulder top of clingy cotton and Lycra that nearly made it difficult to breathe.

With the good weather of late, she had a nice tan. Thus she left her long, shapely legs—much of which were exposed courtesy of the miniskirt—bare. On her feet were white, webbed pumps with enough heel to make her perhaps the tallest person in Sneem. Save one.

He was sitting with his friends in the far corner of the aptly named Blue Boar, when Ruth took a seat at the bar just in time for last call. Purposely she had not phoned up a woman friend to accompany her, and, drink in hand, she now turned to him. In a movement that resembled the swing of a gun carriage—she had been told by an admirer (Ward)—she turned her crossed legs and upper body, revealed in all of its angular completeness, toward the table.

Sipping from the glass, she then raised her head and regarded the man down the shaft of her long, straight nose.

There was a pause in conversation at the table, at other tables, and finally in most of the bar itself, as one person and then another, and yet another realized what was transpiring. Ruth Honora Ann Bresnahan had come to collect "The O'Suilleabhain" from among his mates. They would either now get married or her reputation would be shot in the South Kerry Mountains. For life.

One fella at the table said something that sounded to Ruth like, "Well, Rory, you got a decision to make. Either our good company and a few dozen more pints, or slow death between them two brilliant crackers." A chin was thrust at Bresnahan's legs.

Said another, "My bet is she's got a knife, fork, salt, pepper, and H.P. sauce in that purse. And you're the meal, my man." A hand smacked loudly between O'Suilleabhain's broad shoulders; he did not flinch.

Said a third, "Jasus—if it was me she was after, you could bloody well burn was left of me corpse in the mornin', life being all downhill after that."

O'Suilleabhain had heard enough. Like some ancient hero among his comrades, he stood to claim his prize.

Without taking her eyes off him, Ruth took another sip from the drink and watched him approach, hoping he'd say something like, You look ravishing. Do you know what you did tonight? It was a miracle. You stopped—literally stopped—conversation in the Blue Boar. Let me sit down here. We'll share a drink and preserve the moment.

It was what her "fella," the dark little dapper man from Dublin, whom she had abandoned, would have said, along with endearments enough to win her wholehearted energies for the night.

Instead O'Suilleabhain said, "You look smashin'. C'mon, let's go."

"What about my drink?"

"Leave it. You don't like drink anyway, so."

"Why don't you sit and we'll talk. Here, what are you having?" She reached for her purse.

"What's to talk about? If I wanted a pint, I've got a brace of them backed up at the table."

"But I'd like to finish my drink. I'd like to sit here for a while," and have you chat me up before the eyes of the collected community, went unsaid; and *then* we can leave and *see* what else might occur. Tonight you could be one lucky Culchie buck.

"But it's last call," he insisted.

"It'll be last call until the cock crows." The only strangers in the place were patent tourists, and since it was high summer, the bar would close at the owner's leave. "You know so yourself."

"But I'm ready to go."

"And I just got here."

"More blame you."

Bresnahan raised her glass; there were some things said in life that could not be taken back. That was one. "I've changed my mind, and here's your choice. You can either return to your friends and your pints. Or go home alone. Do I give you the ring back here, or mail it to you in the morning?"

As though having been delivered a blow to the jaw, O'Suilleabhain's head went back. "I don't understand."

She could see that he did. He knew; it was over.

Then, "Why do this . . . *here?*" His eyes roamed the bar and flickered toward the tables where people were still watching them. "You'll ruin my chances altogether." For election to the Dail, he meant.

That was it; he was worried more about his ego and prospects than he was about her and them. How it would play with the fellas; how his reputation would fare. "And think of your mother," he added.

Which was base.

Ruth turned to the barman, who had been loitering not quite out of earshot. "I'd like another drink, please. And whatever this man is having. But deliver it to his table, please."

Next morning she left for Donegal.

# 8

# Things Die

Rossbeg lies eight miles northwest of Ardara on Loughros More Bay. It has a small, shallow, natural harbor, a handful of houses protected from the blasts off the Atlantic by stubby dune hills, and a few piers where fishing boats are docked.

Hal Shevlin lived in the longest one, a low, rambling structure, recently limed, with a bright blue door and matching window frames. An old fishing net—made of plastic and also blue—was holding down the thatch, secured to the ground by stout pegs.

There were four young children playing on the dock, where a sturdy wooden fishing boat of maybe fifty feet was lashed down in a web of lines and heeled over on the low tide. Turk's head bumpers had been slung from the rails of the vessel, and a few of the lines even led out onto the sandy, exposed bottom of the bay. There listed two large mushroom anchors. In all, the house and boat had a battened-down appearance, as though already prepared for the long winter to come. Now in July.

McGarr pulled himself out of his Cooper and staggered in the blast off the bay. It was warm but laden with spray and the briny tang of low tide. The children were wearing yellow oilskins.

"We'll have to mind the wife now," Sergeant Treacy, the local Guard, advised as they moved toward the old Deux Chevaux that was parked by the door. "She has a tongue that could clip a hedge."

There was a battered and strapped suitcase in the back of the car, and a wicker hamper on the passenger seat. The window was open. McGarr lifted the lid to reveal sandwiches wrapped in waxed paper, some carrots and celery stalks in a glassine bag, an apple, an orange, a banana. Somebody was going away.

"Your man," said Treacy as the blue door opened and Hal Shevlin stepped out. Like his children, he too was wearing a fisherman's yellow foul-weather parka, and he was carrying another case. He stopped, seeing them, and glanced at the children, before placing the grip beside the other in the car.

He then turned to them, a square, balding man in his late thirties with a clean-shaven, weather-scoured face and gray eyes, like McGarr's own.

"This is Chief Superintendent Peter McGarr. We'd like a word with you," said Treacy.

"If you can make it fast."

"Going somewhere?" McGarr asked.

"Scotland. I've got the chance of a job." Shevlin turned and, ducking his head under the low door, led them into the house. It was dry, snug, and as bright as the exterior with a new coat of paint on the hallway walls and colorful bric-a-brac mementos from Alaska, Canada, Scotland, and France.

Shevlin opened another door, evidently to the kitchen from the puff of heat and cooking smells that wafted out. "It'll be a few more minutes for the picture, Breege. I've the Guards here at the moment." He moved to close the door, but a small, dark woman appeared there, drying her hands on her apron.

"Oh? Why?"

Shevlin's gray eyes flashed at McGarr, who said, "A few questions about Nellie Millar."

Both Shevlins waited.

"We're trying to understand how she died. And when."

Shevlin moved to open another door, but his wife stopped him. "No—*why*?"

McGarr tried to word his statement indirectly. "We'd like to make sure that her death was accidental."

"And you came here?" Her dark eyes were now bright and hard.

Shevlin pushed open the sitting room door; a kettle in the kitchen began piping.

"Jesus, Mary, and Joseph—a man takes a few fish to feed his children, and there he's marked a criminal for the rest of his days. And now, what? A *murderer*? Hal, here, wouldn't have given that elitist bitch the heat off his water, I'm here to tell you. The common working people of Donegal—farmers and fishermen—are better off with her dead. And that's the truth of it."

Now Shevlin had both men fully in the sitting room, and he began to close the door.

"Don't you be long with them gobshites, Hal—they've got nothing but time, working for the government. And you've that ferry to catch with Larne a half-day off." Larne in Northern Ireland was an embarkation point to Glasgow.

Shevlin closed the door, and they heard the kitchen door slam.

"What's she on about now?" Treacy asked, removing his hat. He was a gray, older man who was close to retirement, and his starched uniform shirt fit him like a loose carapace.

"Only what she should. The old story. We're just trying to survive here, like everybody else."

McGarr looked around the small but comfortable, if tasteless, sitting room, which was packed with an over-stuffed divan and two large chairs to match. It was plain the wife kept the house like a new pin.

There was an old-model telly in one corner, the screen covered by a piece of clear plastic. Every available surface was filled with framed photos or ceramic figurines. A candle was burning in a red crystal devotional shrine on the mantel with a supply of fresh candles in a box nearby. Above the shrine was a saccharine rendering of Jesus Christ bearing his sacred heart.

"The candle will stay lit until I return," explained Shevlin, a bit self-consciously. "It's a family tradition." His having had to be away, either on the water or in foreign parts, McGarr took him to mean. There were further mementos from his travels, as well as photos of other leave-takings when the Shevlins were younger and their children infants and toddlers. In each was a suitcase or a traveling grip.

"May I?" McGarr pointed to one of the stuffed chairs.

Shevlin nodded. "But Breege is right. If I'm not on the Spey tomorrow, they'll give the job to somebody else, and I can't trust the old car."

McGarr was now more than a little interested in the cause of the woman's anger. "Could you run through the 'old story,' quickly?" When Shevlin glanced at Treacy,

McGarr added, "The way it is, we could keep you from leaving altogether—at least for forty-eight hours," which was the option the Garda possessed in interviewing persons when conducting an inquiry into a serious crime.

Treacy nodded.

Shevlin unsnapped his parka. "Tea?"

McGarr shook his head; it might bring the wife back into the room.

"It's the fishing, of course, as Jimmy here can tell you."

"I'd prefer to hear it from you."

Shevlin spread his work-inspissated fingers, then twined them across his chest. "I don't like to go away. Nobody likes to go away. But Donegal men have had to emigrate since the British, and there's no reason for it. Now. Apart from government policy."

McGarr waited; Shevlin's voice was low and gravelly, a kind of toneless rumble.

"Sure, there's plenty of fish in the sea off our shores, and a great market for it worldwide. But Dublin is prohibiting Irish fishermen from taking their share, while permitting the Spanish and Portuguese to 'hammer' every feckin' species they can search out with all the newfangled electronics *their* governments give them. To say nothing of their ships. Convoys of them, some of them big as ocean liners. All subsidized."

McGarr had read about the "hammering" of species. It was now possible with modern electronic gadgets to locate schools of fish and identify them as to species. Using new supernets, fishermen could take all the fish there, leaving almost none of any given school to reproduce. The practice was effectively eliminating certain species from waters where they had been present since men first began to fish.

There were now so few cod off Newfoundland, in Canada, that the Canadian government had declared cod fishers redundant, and were paying them to look for employment in other sectors of the economy. And the Grand Banks there had once been the most prolific fishing ground in the Atlantic, if not the world.

"Why?" The selective enforcement, Shevlin meant. "To trade for Spanish and Portuguese votes on agricultural matters in the E.C. In this country the big farmer rules all. Even when it's pointed out to the government, they say fishing—you know, men in boats, as it was practiced since time immemorial—is passé. Fish *farming*, like the salmon farms that are sprouting up, is the wave of the future, and the big fish *farmers* who can afford to get into it. Sitting on their fat arses in Dublin, those bureaucrats don't give two shits for the people of the West of Ireland, who have been fishing for salmon and sea trout in these bays since before recorded time." Shevlin's face was now even redder.

"But you can't tell us you were fishing traditionally when they took you in, Hal," Treacy said in a soft voice.

"No—damn it, I wasn't. I was just doing what the Spanish and Portuguese are *allowed* to do. Taking our fish. Hell, man—if a species is going to be—*is* being—fished out, who better than by us?

"And Nellie Millar?" Shevlin turned his head to McGarr. "She was worse than any of them in Dublin. She objected to every method of fishing for salmon and sea trout *but* angling. It didn't seem to matter to her that draft-netting—three men in a boat—is a more ancient fishing method in these parts than angling. Angling was the fishing method of the English, which made poaching both a way of putting food on the table and an act of defiance."

McGarr blinked. It was what Shevlin had been doing at the bridge last night and perhaps also on the night Nellie had died. Poaching was a nasty practice, and in Shevlin's case—having been prohibited from drift-netting for salmon—doubly defiant. A heavy, multiply barbed hook was dropped into pools where salmon were known to be lying in number, then yanked out. The fish were gored, some of them straight through, and hauled up into the air. Those that wriggled off the hooks died miserably; McGarr himself had come upon them flailing in agony in shallows.

"But to be fair, Hal," Treacy again said, "it wasn't a bit of poaching that Nellie objected to, but the kind of drift-netting that would make the Owenea and the other salmon rivers of the country like the Erne."

McGarr knew about that too. The Erne River was at one time perhaps the most productive salmon fishery in the world. But in the late 1940s, the Irish government established a hydroelectric facility on the river, and now only stray salmon were caught there. Conclusion? If the returning salmon were not allowed to spawn, in short time there would be no more salmon.

It was plain now that Shevlin was wroth; his eyes were hooded and his ears had pulled back. He still had his fingers twined across his chest, but he was breathing heavily. "You're entitled to your opinion of the woman, and I to mine. But Breege was right. Nellie Millar was an elitist, perfectionist bitch. Before she grassed on me and my little operation out beyond the mouth of the bay, I spoke with her about it. We had it out both then and later in the pages of *Eire Rod and Reel* and that blasted environmentalist newsletter she handed out like every word was from God's mouth.

"She gave me the argument that the well-heeled angler, flying in from New York or Dusseldorf or Toronto, contributes more to the Irish economy for each salmon caught than any net fisherman could hope to produce. There's the cost of the Aer Lingus flight, the rental car, the hotels or

B and Bs, the gasoline, the meals, the pints, the gear, the gifts for the folks back home, the ghillies, the fees for fishing, the whatnot. She might have been a selfish woman, but she was well schooled, and she figured it out. I saw the numbers. She had it that it cost the visiting angler nearly a thousand pounds per salmon taken, if he stayed only two weeks. On the other hand, I might get twenty pounds for a big fish, twenty more to the middleman who sells it here or abroad.

"My reply to her? Who has the better right to an Irish salmon caught in Irish waters, and *whatever* it might bring in? Me—whose people have been fishing here since the Druids, or them shaggers from God knows where who're putting money into the pockets of Aer bloody Lingus, or Hertz rental car, or the tosser who owns the hotel and probably lives in London?

"And it wasn't the Spics and Port-a-gees with all their space-age fish finders that she blew the whistle on—no— but a group of Donegal men who were just trying to support themselves where they were born and brought up. We weren't out hammerin' nothing. We couldn't, we can't. We don't have the gear, which is the long and short of it."

But again Treacy said, "You don't know that she was the one."

"Who else but her, a blow-in herself? Do you know any local who would turn some other local in for taking a few salmon? It wasn't like I was deprivin' anybody. I spread the work out. Anybody who needed a few quid and whose family had fished of old and was willing to work, got work with me.

"And didn't she hire a boat to take her out to see who we were. She took pictures and wrote down my numbers. I watched her do it."

"When?"

"Last year. No, two ago."

"And it took her a year to turn you in?"

Shevlin said nothing.

Asked McGarr: "Did she speak to you about it? Warn you or anything?"

"Only to remind me that I had a quota."

"And you were taking your quota."

Shevlin averted his gaze.

Conclusion: he was taking all the fish he could get—salmon, trout, cod, pollock; any marketable species—so he would not have to go to Scotland or some other place for winter work. It was the way the men here in the West, whose farms were too small to support their families alone, had always fished; if the salmon were running, they fished dawn to dusk and got all they could.

"The fine alone was five thousand pounds. They've prohibited me from using my boat for two years, and I had to beg for that."

"Four nights ago you were poaching by the bridge?" asked McGarr.

There was no reply.

If he had been, he would undoubtedly have seen either Nellie drown or her body floating by. "It's how you knew that Nellie Millar had died before her body was discovered." And why you as much as bragged about that knowledge was equally clear—you hated her and were glad she was dead. McGarr now looked on the man with different eyes.

"I don't know how to ask you this, Hal," said Treacy. "But do you mean to say that you *watched* her die?"

"I didn't *mean* to say anything. And I won't. Apart from the fact that I've seen a lot of things die in my time. Men, women, fish, seals, salmon, cattle. Families." He shrugged, as though to say, What's one more? "Wasn't she trying to kill me and mine?"

"Did you kill her then?" McGarr asked.

"In what way? In not jumping in after her? Man, you must be daft. That river was as high as I've ever seen it, and I'm the engine around this house. Without me, my wife and children might not stand much of a chance. Not with the way things are."

"That's cock and shite, that is," Treacy scoffed. "And you know it, Hal. Wasn't there anything you could have thrown her? You're a fisherman. You've been on boats all your life. Surely you could have done something to save her."

"Well—I wasn't on a boat, was I?"

"What about your poaching line? What test is that?"

"And my barb? Amn't in enough trouble as it is, without gaffing a woman in a stream? And I'm thinking it didn't matter anyhow, from what I later saw. And heard." Shevlin's eyes flickered at McGarr; it was what he had to tell them, and why he had spoken at the bridge last night about what he had termed McGarr's "reenactment" of Nellie's death.

"When I got into town to drop off my fish, wasn't there a light on in her shop, and her bending over her table in the back, wrapping the feathers and so forth, like she did. The flies, you know. Says I to meself, it was an apparition I saw on the Owenea. Or a dream.

"But then"—Shevlin twisted his neck and glanced at the candle flickering in the devotional shrine on the mantel, a wee smile forming at the corners of his mouth"—I had no drink taken, not a drop. And I don't do much dreamin'."

"How did you know it was Nellie inside the shop?" McGarr asked.

"Wasn't she wearing her cap, the one she was never without. You know, with the down-turned brim. Brown, it is. Like a kind of man's fedora but worked over.

"Do y'know"—Shevlin paused and glanced down at his twined fingers—"there's more locks on that shop than on the Bank of Ireland in College Green. Just one of those rods she sold was worth a whole season of poaching, and there she had dozens of them, to say nothing of her other gear."

Now where did that come from and why? McGarr wondered. Had Shevlin at some point contemplated burglarizing the shop? McGarr knew one thing about interviewing—was it?—a suspect. If you were patient, eventually even the hardest type told you what you wished to know. And Shevlin had come to the "telling" part of the interview; McGarr waited.

"And then, after I dropped off me fish, and came back out into the street, didn't I see the Scottish woman by the door of the shop. Says she to me, 'I think I saw her in there, but she won't answer the door. I knocked, she saw me, then switched off the lights.' She—the Scot—said she wanted to buy some flies and a new net. She asked me if I had had any luck and showed me some new flies she said she was about to try."

"Which Scottish woman?"

"The one that was 'in training' with Nellie?" Treacy asked.

Shevlin nodded, and Treacy explained to McGarr. "Niamh Goulding, she calls herself. She come over here to learn about setting herself up with a shop and fishing school on the Spey, the way Nellie had here in Ardara. Bags of money, and a looker with honey-colored hair. But a tyro. Nellie was a good woman with a pound note, and it's said the Goulding woman was paying her a small fortune to break her in. You know, aping Nellie in everything

105

Nellie did right down to them dressing alike. But—"

"She can't fish a bit," Shevlin interrupted. "Her cast—Jasus, I can *toss* a fly farther with me hand. And I have it that she doesn't see very well. Glasses and all.

"Here, just to show you I wasn't dreamin'." He pushed himself out of the overstuffed chair. "I thought I'd wait a bit and sell it. Or maybe even take it to Scotland now and see what I could get for it, needing the money like I do. For the feckin' fine and all. But now that it's murder."

"We didn't say that," Treacy was quick to say.

Shevlin smirked. From a cupboard in one corner of the room, he withdrew a split-cane rod and a reel that said HOUSE OF HARDY on the spindle. As did the rod in smaller, script print near the grip. The rod had been detached into its two parts and wrapped in a sheath of black plastic secured with rubber bands. "It snagged up against the bridge," Shevlin explained. "I found it just about one that morning." He handed it to McGarr. "Who else could afford something, like that? And who else—?"

Would have left it behind, he was about to say, but a corpse.

More to the point of discovering Nellie's murderer, why would a man, who by his own say-so and his wife's obvious panic needed money so desperately, now offer it up? In Scotland he could have had a sweet hello-good-bye deal for, say, two hundred quid that would have left both buyer and seller smiling. To make it seem like he was telling the truth and had nothing to hide?

"How did you know it was Nellie in the water when she went by you at the bridge?" It was dark, and she or her body must have bolted by the bridge. McGarr himself had felt the force of the river when its current was less strong than on the night she died.

Shevlin did not answer immediately. He sat back down. "Well, now—I assumed it was her, having seen her earlier, like. And who else wears all them fancy togs?"

In the dark with her in the tannin-stained water, it would have been impossible to tell one tog from another.

"No—it was her hair, that's it. Her blond-white hair. She'd lost the hat, don't you know. Or at least I assumed she'd lost the hat. But then, of course, didn't I see her in the shop with it on." His thick fingers raked the air before coupling again across his chest. "I dunno, I'm not a cop. I leave that up to you, like I said, now that it's murder."

"When did you first see her at the river, early that night?" McGarr asked.

"From the moment she arrived. With the Yank."

"Where were you?"

"Let's just say . . . around."

"And what did she do?"

"Hal!" his wife now roared at the door, thumping it once. "The ferry! That job of work!"

Had she been listening? Without a doubt.

Shevlin sighed and looked away, as though beset. "Like I was saying, the Yank took his gear and walked across the road and up the far bank of the river. But she waited, like I was, for the big fish. Just about dark, she returned to the Yank's Rover, suited up, and then moved up the river from the bridge."

"How do you know it was the Yank's car?"

"I walked by it. All her gear was laid out and the dome light left on."

"Her waders?" McGarr watched Shevlin's eyes closely.

He looked away. "I don't know. I guess so. I can remember saying to meself, The dutiful Yank. He'd make a good body servant."

McGarr couldn't keep his nostrils from flaring. "And when you returned from town, was the Yank's car still there?"

"No—his was parked down by Nancy's. The pub, you know. Hers was in the car park by the bridge. It's a Rover too, but new and something that few in these parts can afford."

McGarr thought for a moment. "Who'd you sell your fish to—Nancy's?"

"I wouldn't say, if I could remember. But I hear there's pubs and cafés that will take all the fish they can get, smoking what they don't sell fresh in dinners and the like."

McGarr glanced at Treacy, who nodded.

"But I was in there, in Nancy's, like for a pint."

"That morning?"

Shevlin nodded.

"The Yank there?"

Shevlin shook his head. "But he had been. The barman tried to get me down in price, saying there was a glut of fresh fish, and the rate had fallen."

"The Scottish woman—she lived with Nellie?"

Shevlin's eyes darted toward the door. "I haven't the slightest idea where she lived or lives. Or who with. For my money, she's a bit of a hag."

It was then the door flew open and slapped against a doorstop, rattling the pane of patterned, frosted glass. "Right now—up, up, the three of yez. Me husband's leavin' for Scotland this minute, and you're leavin' my house. Now!"

McGarr glanced at Shevlin, who regarded the woman for a moment, but he stood.

McGarr did as well, but he said to Shevlin, "This might come as a bit of a blow, but I'm going to have to ask you not to leave the country."

"What?" the wife demanded, hands on hips, her jaw set belligerently. "You can't do that. You're not even with the Guards anymore. It was in all the papers."

"Well, then, he can." McGarr canted his head toward Treacy.

"But he wouldn't."

Treacy cleared his throat, and his eyes—shadowed under bushy gray brows—met hers. "Oh, but I would. I will. And why chance the long trip to Larne, only to be turned back? There'll be other jobs."

"In a pig's arse, there will. He's taking *this* job. Hal"— she turned to her husband—"by the time you get yourself there, I'll have this thing sorted out. We're not without our own well-placed friends, you know. In Dublin."

McGarr turned to follow Treacy down the low hallway toward the front door, Nellie's rod and reel in his hand.

"Wait! Stop! Where're you going with that?" she went on. "Don't tell me you gave that dodger the effing rod? You amadan, you. That's salvage, that is. Where in the name of hell was her name? Not on the shaft, not on the reel. Not anywhere."

In a low, even voice, Shevlin said, "I'm going to say this once and once only to you, woman. Shut your gob."

But she went on. "I won't have you out all night with who knows who, who knows where, coming home to me with no money and trouble on you."

Even through the closed door and thick walls of the cottage, they heard a resounding slap. And another. And another.

McGarr and Treacy stopped, before the older man said, "She comes into town every so often, all black-and-blue. When I ask her if it's anything I should concern myself with, she tells me to feck off."

The two men proceeded on to McGarr's Cooper. Glancing in the rearview mirror as they pulled away, McGarr noticed that the four children on the dock had quit their play. Standing in a group, they seemed to be listening to whatever further sounds were now coming from the house.

# 9

## Gear

By the time Sergeant Treacy and McGarr arrived back in Ardara, the intersection on the hilltop was clogged with cars in three directions. Others were parked up on the footpaths.

"Locals, mostly, attending Nellie's funeral." Treacy pointed to the crowd that had gathered to climb the stairs to the church. "I don't care what Shevlin said, Nellie Millar was well respected. She was generous, and there wasn't anything she wouldn't do for you herself, if you were in need."

Except if you were a drift-netter and poacher, McGarr thought, wondering if Nellie had turned the man in. Somehow it didn't sound like the woman he had known. Nellie had seemed to accept the world as it was, and to believe in live and let live. "Who fingered Shevlin?"

"Dunno. I don't think anybody does. I asked the government men who came to impound Shevlin's boat. The man in charge would only say it was anonymous. But whether that's policy—" Treacy hunched his thin shoulders. "But he had a letter, the boat's numbers, and photographs that placed Shevlin and the boat where they shouldn't have been. Not once, but day after day after day. There must've been two dozen pics all on different days."

Motive enough for a man, like Shevlin, who had—what was the phrase?—seen many *things* die, by his own dispassionate admission? A man who was violent with women and, given his needs, would have considered the seizure of his boat, the fine, and the proscription against fishing for two years a massive, personal affront. Then there was the anomaly in regard to the time of Nellie's death.

Had Shevlin's purpose, in speaking to him at the bridge and suggesting that Nellie had died earlier than first thought, been to point up that she had in fact been murdered, albeit it craftily? And by him? Would he have wanted somebody, anybody, even the police to know that he had gotten his revenge?

Plainly McGarr did not know enough, but the discrepancy in regard to the chronology of her death bothered him mightily. And he knew this: murderers almost always tried too hard to cover up their crime. They made mistakes.

What did he have? So far, he had Shevlin saying she died shortly after midnight, but that then—miraculously—he saw her in her fishing shop, tying a fly at her vise. Stearns had said that too. And Shevlin added that he had seen and spoken to a Scottish woman, one Niamh Goulding, who also said she saw Nellie in her shop. She would have to be questioned.

Also, there was the question of who had access to Nellie's waders and when. Earlier in Stearns's Rover, which—as Shevlin reported—had been open with Nellie's gear laid out and the dome light on? Or later, after she returned from her shop? If earlier, either Stearns or Shevlin could have cut them, but would Shevlin have known Nellie was intending to wade? Probably not, given the terms they were on. And Stearns said he couldn't understand why she had chosen to wade.

Could they have been cut on the offchance that she would? It was a possibility, but McGarr did not think so. Had they been cut and she had not waded, she most probably would have discovered the breach, and the opportunity of using that method again would be gone. Also, she would have been alerted to the fact that somebody was intent on doing her harm.

Then there were the Rovers. Or, rather, the two Land Rovers—one old, one new. If Nellie had died when Shevlin intimated she had, how did her new-model vehicle come to be found at the car park by the bridge. "Nellie's Rover was locked," McGarr said aloud, going over what he knew.

"Tighter than a drum," said Treacy. "When I phoned her father in Mayo and told him about Nellie, he asked me to bring the car round to the house. When I found it locked, my first thought was the undertaker—you know, Nellie would have had the keys on her, like. Failing that, I went up to the house, thinking there'd be a set someplace there. The front door was open, but I couldn't find anything that looked like a car key. When her father arrived, we finally found a set in the fly shop."

Which was strange. Nellie would have either zipped them into her fishing parka or into the pouch under the bib in the waders. And no place else. Fighting a salmon often took much strenuous effort, and things slung into a pocket could fall out. And Nellie had been careful about such things.

Said Treacy, "It occurred to me that she might have lost them in the river. But I do a bit of angling myself, and I batten my key ring down good, just on the offchance of a tumble or a spill."

"But would she have taken her keys with her when she went fishing with the Yank?" McGarr asked aloud.

Treacy thought for a moment. Still stalled in the heavy traffic, they could now hear the church bell ringing. "Maybe not, if she didn't intend to return to her shop. Not having her own Rover, she wouldn't have need for them."

Then without keys, how did she get the car out to the car park? Also, how did she get the mile into town with all her gear in the dead of night? Walk? Perhaps, but somebody was sure either to have seen her or to have given her a lift.

As though reading McGarr's mind, Treacy said, "I'll put out the word about anybody seeing her on the road. Ardara's a small place, and it'll soon be everywhere."

Along with the suspicion of murder, McGarr thought. But after the interview with Shevlin and his harridan of a wife, there was no help for that now. Ruth Bresnahan could not arrive too soon.

"What about this Stearns fella?" McGarr now asked.

"The Yank."

He nodded. If his Rover had been parked in front of Nancy's Pub, but he was not in the pub when Shevlin arrived with his fish, where was he? Not at home—how would he have gotten there? And the Yank wife or whatever—Jane Trowbridge—had as much as said he was not. "What was his relationship to Nellie?"

"Shevlin had it right—body servant, I should imagine."

"Where would he have spent the night after he left Nancy's?"

Treacy shook his head. "He gets around, I'd say. Oftentimes I see his old banger parked here and there around the village early enough to make it all night." He waved his hand at the windscreen. "Lots of tourists about this time of year. Single women from the North mostly—schoolteachers, career women—and the odd German or Dutch woman, looking for a bit of a fling. He's something . . . different, I'd say. Looking the way he does. The cowboy hat and silver boots and so forth. There's many a local lass thinks he's 'gear,' I believe the word is."

It was, at least in Dublin; it was also street slang for heroin. "What about the wife and kids he's got out in Maghera?"

"He tells everybody who'll listen to him she's *not* his wife."

Officially, thought McGarr; again he wondered what Nellie had ever seen in the lout. "What do you think?"

"Who might have slit her waders?" Treacy shook his head. "I don't know what to think. Yet."

# PART III

We catch fish, when we bait our hooks with our hearts.

—HENRY DAVID THOREAU

# 10

# A Silver Trout

The main door of the little church was at the rear, and McGarr had to walk through the churchyard to approach it. There his eye caught on a freshly dug grave with a new stone and the name MILLAR cut in the granite, which demonstrated at least that Nelson Millar was still in charge of the details of his life. And Nellie's death.

McGarr glanced at the open door, where people were standing. He could push through the crowd and listen to the practiced tones of the minister, which were partially audible, or he could stand where Nellie's remains would rest and await the others. From there he would have a good view of the church door, and who was there and who not.

And then, from the little he could hear of the eulogy, it sounded like the cosmetic makeup had looked on Nellie's face—lurid, an indignity. He stepped toward the stone, which was on a high part of ground that commanded a good view of the town, the bay beyond, and the Slieve Tooey in the distance. Like a coded message, dots and dashes of brilliant white cloud were arrayed in a line out over the ocean; otherwise the sky was the pale color of a robin's egg.

The years of her life had been inscribed on the stone, along with an inscription. McGarr stepped closer.

> I will find out where she has gone,
> And kiss her lips and take her hands;
> And walk among long dappled grass,
> And pluck till time and times are done
> The silver apples of the moon,
> The golden apples of the sun.
>
> W. B. YEATS

"It's from 'The Song of Wandering Aengus,' " Noreen, McGarr's wife, said from behind him. He turned, and Maddie came rushing to him, her arms stretched out. "Daddy!"

McGarr picked her up, twirled her around, and kept her in his arms. "What's an Aengus?"

"It's the Irish Eros, the god of love, youth, and beauty. You know the poem, don't you?"

McGarr shook his head.

"The speaker of the poem has a fire in his head. He cuts a hazel wand and hooks a berry to a thread. Shall I recite the rest?"

McGarr glanced toward the church door, where people were now just beginning to come out; it would be their own little ceremony, he judged. "Please."

> "And when the white moths were on the wing,
> And moth-like stars were flickering out,

## Death on a Cold, Wild River

I dropped the berry in a stream
And caught a little silver trout.

"When I had laid it on the floor
I went to blow the fire aflame,
But something rustled on the floor,
And some one called me by my name;
It had become a glimmering girl
With apple blossom in her hair
Who called me by my name and ran
And faded through the brightening air.

"Though I am old with wandering
Through hollow lands and hilly lands,

"And then the rest that you see there."

McGarr himself read the balance of the poem aloud, ostensibly to Maddie but more for himself—to get the sense of it, to ... participate.

"I will find out where she has gone,
And kiss her lips and take her hands;
And walk among long dappled grass,
And pluck till time and times are done
The silver apples of the moon,
The golden apples of the sun."

"A silver trout, of course, is a salmon," Noreen explained. "In Irish mythology it's the salmon, rather than the serpent, that is the main symbol of immortality. You know, the leap of the salmon being the leap of inspiration, the salmon's epic sexual energy, its return and renewal every blessed year without fail, its nimbleness."

McGarr regarded his wife, whose powers of analysis and

121

command of the culture of the country always amazed him. She forgot nothing.

Like a bright auburn bird turning an ear to the ground, she had inclined her head toward the inscription, her arms folded neatly at her waist in her characteristic "thinking posture," McGarr thought of it affectionately.

She was well tanned—or, rather, freckled—from the sunny weather that Dublin had enjoyed since late spring, and McGarr could see that she had taken pains to wear the new dark summer suit that she had bought on her shopping spree in Dublin a few weeks earlier. It made the most of her trim but angular figure and sleek legs. Her green eyes flashed as she lifted her head.

"Also, the elusiveness of the salmon, which is the point of the poem. How many times have I heard you come home from fishing saying, 'Oh, they were there all right. You could see them leaping. The trick is in catching them.' But then you add, 'But, sure, the point of fishing is not just catching fish.' It's the pursuit, the quest."

And being out-of-doors, McGarr thought. Nellie once told him it wouldn't matter if she had nothing—no wordly goods or possessions—as long as she was out on a stream, a river, or a lake.

"Shall I continue?" Noreen asked.

"Yes, luveen, do. I was going to ask yez what yeh think it means," said an old, shawl-draped woman who now joined them.

Noreen flashed her a welcoming smile. "One reading of the poem would have the salmon—which turns into a girl, who then eludes the speaker—symbolizing occult knowledge. Or perhaps, as applied to Nellie Millar, the impossibility of knowing the natural world in all its particularity, as rewarding as a lifelong attempt to gain that knowledge might be. Of course, the entire poem relates to the legend of Fionn mac Cumhaill," she pronounced in her excellent Irish.

"Is that Finn MacCool?" Irish had never been one of McGarr's better subjects when in school.

"Surely you of all people, you who has caught your share of salmon, knows the legend of Fionn and the Salmon of All Knowledge?" Noreen asked with no little academic horror. "Fionn's monolith is right here in Ardara. His wife's tomb, the *Teach Mor*, is nearby in *Gill na mBan*. Don't you remember the intro I wrote to that volume of *Irish Antiquities* that Rizzoli published, oh"—she had to think—"six or seven years ago?"

McGarr did not. Noreen was always working on some fine arts project that he little understood. But he nodded. Over his shoulder Maddie was studying the dark, stony interior of the freshly dug grave.

Said the old woman, "Fionn's stone is that big standing stone by the bridge over the Owenea. The massive thing."

"Twelve feet high, four-sided, with two small cup marks, as I remember."

"The very thing."

"Legend has it that Fionn tossed it there from the top of *Cro-na-cleire*. You know, as a boundary stone."

"Marking off what Fionn controlled. It would be his way, sure it would." The crone was smiling now, warming to the story. "I heard it all said often at my father's hearth."

"Anyhow, where was I?" Noreen looked around, distracted.

"Finn and the salmon," said McGarr, remembering—again vaguely from school—that Finn and his gang were a rough lot of tossers and bowsies. They spent their time boozing, brawling, and bragging, with the odd session beside a woman merely to round out their experience and provide for a next generation of toughs.

"It happened right here in Donegal on the Erne, or so some think. As a lad, Fionn and Bran, his magical dog, took shelter in a great sea cave. In came an enormous Druid Cyclops carrying the Salmon of All Knowledge, which he had been trying to catch for centuries."

"To get the knowledge, don't you know," the old woman chorused. "Everything took forever back then."

"Tired from his struggle with the fish, the Cyclops handed it to Fionn and ordered him to cook it for him while he napped. But he warned Fionn that, if in any way he burned the fish, he would eat Fionn too."

"And wouldn't you know, up came a blister on the salmon the moment the Druid closed his eye."

Noreen nodded. "Fionn tried to press it down with his thumb, which he burned."

"And into his gob it went along with the knowledge that the Druid wished to get for himself."

"From that moment forward, Fionn only ever had to gnaw on his thumb to know what was about to happen." Noreen looked up and blinked; she was finished.

"But whatever happened to Finn in the cave?" McGarr asked in a low tone, now that the church had emptied and others were gathering about them.

Said the old woman, "Since he knew what to do, didn't Fionn blind the bugger with a blazin' brand from the fire. But the Druid got to the mouth of the cave and said he'd never let them out. Our Fionn lad, though, nibbled his knuckle and then killed two of the goats that was in the cave. Disguising himself and his mutt in their fleeces, Fionn slipped away in the morning with the goats that were being let out to graze."

The old woman turned to Noreen. "Tell me, you who knows so much. What does Fionn mac Cumhaill mean?"

"White Cap," said Noreen without hesitation.

"Just like our poor Nellie," said the old woman. "She was the very best. And a lover of salmon, like Fionn. Are yeh a teacher?"

Noreen shook her head.

"Well, you should be. Yeh tell it grand."

The casket had appeared in the door of the church, and the people around them grew quiet.

McGarr scanned the crowd, but there was no Hank Stearns. He handed Maddie to Noreen. "The key is at the desk of the hotel. It's at the corner where the roads cross."

"Where will you be?"

"Either in Nancy's Pub or Nellie's fly shop, just across the street."

Nancy's Pub was down the hill from the church, and rather than buck the traffic, which was still backed up as far as the eye could see, McGarr walked. Even the footpaths were thronged, mainly with tourists who were window-shopping before the many shops that offered Donegal tweeds, knits, and other craft products. Few of the tourists were speaking English.

The sun was now strong and hot. McGarr doffed his blazer and nudged back his hat. He had to step out into the street to walk past the ornate wrought-iron benches in front of Nancy's; they were filled with other tourists, most holding pints of golden lager in their hands, with the odd Guinness being tasted by the brave.

Stearns's battered red Land Rover was parked up on the footpath by the bridge and was part of the cause of the traffic jam. Unable to get by, an articulated lorry was stalled on the bridge, its driver nowhere to be seen. Sergeant Treacy should give the bastard a ticket, McGarr thought. A brace of them.

The fug inside Nancy's hit McGarr like a hot blast, as

he stepped into a low, shadowed hallway that led to the bar proper on one side and a series of lounges on the other. The smell was a compound of tobacco and peat smoke, doubtless left over from the fires of last night, which probably had never gone out, and the acridly sweet aroma of porter, whiskey, and beer.

More a large shebeen than a pub, Nancy's was a warren of small rooms so low that a tall man had to mind the transoms. Each tiny lounge had its own fireplace and was furnished with armchairs, love seats, and benches, like a miniature parlor. In them strangers were often thrown together, McGarr knew from his own experience there years ago, while the younger people of the town at that time, preferring their own select company, had chosen to stand in the dark hall where they could order their pints over a Dutch-door serving counter.

Little had changed. Easing his way through a gaggle of young ones, McGarr finally made the door of the bar, and that of the first lounge across from it. Seated there on a long bench against the wall was a woman whom he had seen at the funeral earlier. She looked enough like a younger Nellie Millar to hold his interest. Facially, at least.

Her features were fair and regular with the same high cheekbones and high forehead that Nellie had possessed. And even her hair was blond, albeit a golden honey color. Yet she was taller than Nellie, and her eyes were blue.

She was wearing a cotton summer jumper that was also blue over a khaki fishing blouse and a khaki skirt. There were touches of yellow gold—in her earrings, an expensive-looking sports watch, a wedding band, and the band of an engagement ring that displayed a diamond the size of a collar stud. There was also gold in the chain that held a pair of sunglasses that were hanging from her neck.

Her legs were crossed away from the low table in front

of her. On it were two drinks, both large whiskeys—hers light, like some good-quality Scotch; the other drink dark but not reddish, like brandy or bourbon. Noticing McGarr staring at her, she reached for her sunglasses. McGarr stepped into the bar proper.

It too was a small, dark room with a patterned tin ceiling and a serving bar cramped into a corner. Every available space had been employed, and the bottles and tins of cigars and packets of cigarettes were packed to the ceiling. Antiques and nautical, fishing, and other curios were tucked here and there or hanging from the ceiling. A man with a fiddle, another with a guitar, and a third playing a bodhran occupied the far seats. Obviously they had just finished a set, since there had been music playing when McGarr was in the hallway, and now some of the tourists in the crowded bar were leaving. But no Stearns.

McGarr ordered a Powers neat, pulled up a stool, and sat. When he turned and looked out the door of the bar into the sitting room opposite, the woman was gone. But not the fresh drinks. McGarr kept his eyes on them.

A minute or so later, Stearns appeared from the other end of the hall where the jakes was located, McGarr seemed to remember. Stearns began to turn into the room but stopped, his tall, spare frame filling the door. He then peered up the hall and even stepped outside, before checking the bar.

Seeing McGarr, he hesitated for a moment before turning on his smile. "If it ain't," he said. "But it is." He ambled forward in an aw-shucks manner, hat on head, arms akimbo. His curling upper lip, fringed by the blonding moustache, revealed a reach of perfect teeth. In his tanned face they seemed very white: the blue-green eyes beamed down on McGarr. "Hot one, hey? Been up at the church?" Like most Americans, his twangy voice was too loud.

McGarr nodded.

"Couldn't make it myself. That whole funeral scene gives me the creeps. Anyways, I said my good-byes to Nellie the last couple days. I couldn't bear seeing her in a box, and then all that dirt." He shook his head. "Not Nellie, who had so much . . . life, know what I'm saying?"

Again McGarr could barely keep his outrage at what he was hearing—the words, the tone of voice, the offhand manner, even the way the man carried himself in his bloody cowboy costume—from getting the better of him. He had to tell himself that the person he was listening to was no more from Montana than he was himself, that he was a Ph.D. stream entomologist and failed university teacher from urban-industrial, northeast Ohio, and there was some reason for the disguise and the act. McGarr had a cousin who had emigrated to Youngstown.

"Wanna drink?"

McGarr glanced down at his own glass, which was empty.

"Charlie—give our gumshoe friend here another snort. And me, I'll have one too. When you get a chance. Please."

That was it, McGarr decided—it didn't matter what Stearns said, even if polite, it was his tone that grated. It was condescending and dismissive, as if nothing and nobody he was dealing with was important; laid-back, Stearns was just going through the motions. Of life—being alive himself. Know what I'm saying?

"But Hank"—the barman glanced across the hall and into the sitting room,—"you have a drink in there. I just put it down."

Stearns did not turn to look.

"But sure, if you want another, I'll pour it. It's why I'm here. You're the boss." There was a note of humorous derision in that, and the barman's eyes met McGarr's, as though sharing it.

"Was that Niamh Goulding sitting in there?" McGarr asked.

"What if it was? She was a friend of Nellie's too. She even went to the funeral." Stearns's tone was now defensive.

"And left in a hurry. There, and here just now."

Stearns picked up the glass that the barman placed before him. "You mean, when she saw you walk in?" He chuckled. "Little fella—I ain't drunk, like I was the last time we spoke. And from what I hear, you ain't nobody special anymore. Did it ever dawn on you that I'm just tryin' to be personable, buying you a drink like this? Or that the lady might be coming back?"

As she now did, placing a hand on the jamb of the bar doorway and smiling at Stearns as though to say, Sorry,—I'm back. Niamh Goulding then turned and sauntered into the sitting room to resume her seat there, her step lithe and springy, her hands even flouncing her skirt in a little-girlish manner that collected the eyes of a few of the young men in the hallway.

"I mean, it's time for you to get real about yourself and your Sam Spade routine. You're not a cop anymore, and nothing cop-related happened here anyways. It was an accident, and you should try and forget it. So you once knew Nellie. So did I. . . . " He abandoned the thought. "But drop it. Nobody likes a noodge."

It was all McGarr could do to control himself. His blood was pounding in his temples, and his heart was beating in his throat. He had to force himself to say, "Why don't you introduce me? We'll have the drink together."

Stearns drank off his in one swallow and dropped the glass on the bar. "Some other time—we're busy now."

"About what? She the one who gave you the sterling bank notes?"

Stearns's eyes fell on him again. "Like I said, pal—don't press your luck. Charlie, put the drinks on my tab." Stearns turned to the door. There he had to duck and ease himself through. The young people in the hallway parted to let him into the sitting room. He said something that made them laugh.

Resuming his seat by the woman, Stearns smiled at her and she stared at him, as though sharing a joke. Not exactly unlike lovers, McGarr judged.

Stearns with the nonwife and three children out in the 'shieling' in Maghera. Stearns who "got around" with women by Sergeant Treacy's report; Stearns for whom women were "the thing."

"Sure, it could have been worse," said the barman from the pad where he was noting down Stearns's charges. "Sometimes he calls me Chazz, which at least rhymes with jazz. Other times it's *Chuck.*" He winced and shook his head.

# 11

# A Hackle of
# Jungle Cock

Once back outside, McGarr glanced up the street toward the church on the hill. The funeral was just breaking up. He moved quickly across the street toward the fly shop, since Nellie's name would still be on every tongue, and the Ardara rumor mill was doubtless a potent enough engine on its own.

There were three stout locks on the sturdy front door of the shop—two dead bolts, one high, one low; and an automatic latch on the doorknob. The small bay display window was both wired and secured with a steel mesh. Behind it was a collection of antique rods and reels, their make, model, and date of manufacture described on neat, intaglio nameplates.

Stepping in, McGarr had to put his shoulder against the door and push. Piled on the floor was the mail that the shop had received in the short week since Nellie's death. Much of it was foreign and contained in envelopes that appeared to be from a catalog or mailing that Nellie had sent out. The fly-shop address was printed, and Nellie's leaping-salmon logo was on the back flap. The volume of the responses gave McGarr an idea of the success of her enterprise here in Ardara.

Without touching the inner door handle, he let the door swing back on itself, not wishing to touch anything that he found in the shop. He looked up.

The shop was long and narrow with a bank of multiply paned windows looking out over the Owentocker River, which flowed past the south wall of the building. Like the bar across the street, every available space had been put to use. There were rods of every description—salmon, trout, pike, even spinning and surf-casting varieties— either lined on hangers from the ceiling or bristling from rod holders on the display floor.

One aisle was devoted to fishing lines, leaders, and tippet material; another, which was an immense case, to reels. A third aisle to fishing accessories, such as stream boots, waders, implements—snips, forceps, jacket-lights, knives, creels, priests, gaffs, nets, etc.

The inventory was impressive, especially the section that contained fly-dressing materials. McGarr's eyes swept over rolls of tinsels, glassine bags of feathers of every sort, others of herl, fur, hair from various animals—caribou, elk, deer, polar bear—the choice went on and on. An octagon case on a swivel in the middle of the shop offered hooks from all the manufacturers that McGarr had ever heard of. And three others he had not.

He turned to the long continuous case of already dressed flies that lined the entire length of the shop beneath the bright, river windows. The collection was about evenly divided between trout and salmon flies, which were larger and far more colorful. The intent in dressing a trout fly was usually that of imitating some creature in nature, for instance—McGarr glanced down—midsummer emergers.

Emergers were mayfly nymphs that had begun their trip from the bed of a stream or river, where they had been hiding, to the surface, where they would shuck their nymphal casings, free their wings, and fly off to mate. At certain times of the year, emergers were a prime trout food. And here again Nellie offered every type that McGarr knew of and many more, each identified by common name, classification, and number. A small sign asked the patron to refer to the number and not remove any flies from the case.

The salmon flies, being almost exclusively "attractors," were brilliant patterns of extravagant color that fishers had discovered salmon would "take" in spite of their distaste for food. McGarr noticed that the glass covering the bank of cases was U.-V.–protected. That alone must have cost—he glanced up—he didn't know. Lots.

His eyes caught on other advisements that were also behind glass, but framed, and hung at various places in the shop. McGarr did not read them all, but one said,

> *I do not merely fish for fish, I fish for doubt's anodyne and care's surcease.*
> *There is no music in a rest, but there is the making of music in it.*

Another,

> *There is nothing more destructive of romance than to think you can take life by the throat and force it to surrender its bounties. Life is not organized that way. After all, the good things come from within not without.*

# A Hackle of Jungle Cock

Yet another,

> My ambition is to be the sort of woman who can endure her own company. And survive.

And still another, prophetically,

> When fishing "stilly" rapid waters, always work against the current, casting over the shoulders of the trout. Don't fight the stream.

Over the fly-tying table, was a quote from Lee Wulff:

> The angler, who wants the exact fly order after order, must stick to the same fly maker or to a limited few, who have no need to substitute for any of the required materials, and always tie in the same manner.

The table itself—where Nellie had last been seen on the night of her death (and *after* Hal Shevlin placed the time of her drowning)—was at the very back of the shop. There, McGarr imagined, she would not have been bothered by traffic noise or customers entering the shop to browse. Fly-tying required steady hands, patience, and no little concentration, to say nothing of skill.

When dressing a fly, McGarr could think of nothing else but the wrapping of thread, feathers, floss, and hair on a hook. Much to his surprise, he had found the activity deeply relaxing, especially after a people-filled workday. He imagined the professional fly-tier might find the practice somewhat less rewarding. But then, the Nellie he had known had taken much pleasure in small details.

Across from the table was a desk where, it appeared, she had conducted the business of the shop. There was a cash register along with a computer, a laser printer, filing cabinets, and a fax machine. McGarr turned his attention to the fly-tying table.

More a kind of large country doctor's desk with a tall top of drawers labeled from A—Avon Eagle Feathers—to Z—Zebra Mane Hair—it too was covered with a variety of implements and materials in a kind of creative jumble that reflected the variety of fly under construction.

There were scissors of various sizes and shapes, hackle pliers of three different kinds, tweezers, a knife, thread on a bobbin, a bodkin for picking out dubbing, jars of head cement and varnish. And finally, there was a vise, a mechanism to hold the hook steady while the other materials were being applied. As in everything else, Nellie's was the best—a Poloma fly-tying lathe.

Trained on the head of the vise was the bead of a strong light. Close by was a large magnifying glass on a stanchion, which seemed odd for Nellie, whose eyes—when McGarr had known her—were sharper than his own. But he suspected that age and her having spent so much time out-of-doors might have dimmed her eyesight. Of late he himself had been having to hold fine print farther and farther away from his eyes to read, and the inevitable appointment with the ophthalmologist was not far off.

The J, C, and F drawers of the upper, alphabetized, materials cabinet were partially open, as were the storage drawers that were clustered under the fly-tying table.

With the end of his fountain pen, McGarr snapped on the vise light. The fly that was clamped in the jaws was a partially completed Jock Scot, a classic salmon-fly pattern that was one of the most difficult to tie. The use of original materials—Indian crow, black ostrich, toucan, gallina, white-tipped turkey tail, swan, bustard, florican, cinnamon and gray turkey tail, peacock sword, "right" and "left" strips of teal, barred summer duck, and brown mallard—created a magnificent fly.

It was so different from the modern equivalent, which was made with dyed or manmade materials. He judged that its brilliant luminosity would not be lost in the water nor its "feel," which was of course natural, in the mouth of a salmon. It was the point of salmon attractors.

Situated beyond the vise, with barbs stuck into a cork fly-holding rail, were three other Jock Scot flies. They were also incomplete, each needing to have its blue-chatterer cheeks and jungle-cock sides attached before the topping and horns were tied in. The fourth fly there had been finished.

McGarr heard a rap on the front door. He turned. It was Noreen and Maddie. "We thought we should discover what you were about. Oh—isn't this place brilliant. God, look at all the stuff. I bet you couldn't find a place like this in Dublin."

Or London, or New York, McGarr thought, but then by mail Nellie had been marketing the world. He advised them not to touch anything, then he said to Noreen, "You can help me. I'm going to switch on the lights at the tying table. I want you to sit in the chair and pretend you're tying a fly. Here—" He walked to the sports clothing section of the shop and selected a hat for her. "—Put this on." It was of a type that he had seen in Nellie's closet and in the photograph of her with Stearns.

"Hat. Can I have a hat too?" Maddie asked.

McGarr gave her one, then took himself outside the shop onto the footpath where, at the bay window, he waited until Noreen had positioned herself at the vise. Granted, it was a midsummer afternoon with a full sun, but even with his eyes that were especially good seeing at a distance, he could make out only that the figure at the table was a woman.

Her back was, of course, turned. But there was the woman's hat, the shape of her upper body, but most telling was the size of her forearm, wrist, and hand, as Noreen pretended to wrap thread around the hook directly under the beam of the vise light.

"Can I help you with something, Peter?" a man's voice said, startling McGarr.

He straightened up; it was Nelson Millar.

McGarr's hand went out to him. "Yes, you can," he said, before remembering that the older man would have missed him at the funeral. "I was there, earlier. At the grave," he began to apologize, "but—"

"I saw you, sure I did. How can I help you?"

"If you'll just step into the shop."

Back at the fly-tying table, McGarr pointed to the fly that was still in the vise, and then at the three other Jock Scots stuck in the cork. "Why wouldn't Nellie have finished off the four flies?"

Nelson Millar had to take out a pair of bifocals and then study the incomplete Jock Scots. "You mean, where are the jungle-cock sides and the blue-chatterer cheeks? And the topping and horns, of course, which only can be added after." He straightened up. "I don't know—a whim? Perhaps she ran out of something? Not blue chatterer, for there it is." Millar pointed down at the sky-blue wax wing feathers on the tying table.

"I checked the J box, but none of its compartments contain jungle cock." It then occurred to McGarr that the C and F boxes had also been left partially open, as though somebody had searched through them as well—C for cock, F for fowl. Jungle Fowl was the general common name for the bird, a cock being the male of the species.

Nelson Millar's head went back. "Oh—it should have occurred to me immediately. Jungle cock—like the toucan, florican, Indian crow, bustard, swan, and so many of the other 'exotic' fly-tying materials—is extremely difficult and expensive to obtain. Most are either endangered species or would be, were governments to allow legal hunting. the case of jungle cock, we have what is called an 'endangered species.' If a fly-tier is discovered tying with jungle cock, he or she has to prove that he's obtained the feathers legitimately and not from some poacher or on the black market." Millar read the question in McGarr's eyes. "By that I mean, he must have an Endangered Species Import Licence attesting to the fact that those birds were hatched, raised, and died in captivity, or the feathers were molted from captive-bred populations.

"As a committed environmentalist, Nellie was very particular about complying with the requirements. It made the flies she tied from these genuine materials inordinately expensive, but there's a market for them—mainly as display items. You know, to be framed or encased for exhibition in, say, a sportsman's den."

McGarr nodded; he had a few like that hanging on the walls of his own den back in Dublin.

"But, alas, we obtained our supply of gray jungle cock before all this carry-on. One of my fishing friends, who had business in India, came back with an empty sample case simply packed with capes of jungle cock. It was years ago, and he's long dead. But I cared for it properly."

As in everything, McGarr thought.

"When Nellie opened up the shop here, I let her have most of it. I imagine she kept it in the safe, though I'm not certain." The tall, older man, who was dressed in a black suit, moved toward the office area. He pulled back the desk and touched the trim of the wainscoting; a panel in the wood opened up.

"Nellie kept it in here." He pointed to a small safe that was exposed there. "The European Community has become very strict about importing exotic feathers, and, if it had gotten out that she had an undocumented supply, they could have closed her down and confiscated the contents of the place, to say nothing of fines.

"I have the combination here someplace in my billfold, but I'm afraid I left my glasses back at Nellie's." With hands that, McGarr could not help but notice, were quaking, Nelson removed a small card and handed it to McGarr. It was one of Nellie's business cards with a series of numbers written on the back.

McGarr switched on the office lights and squatted down in front of the safe. He dialed in the numbers; the door opened on his second try.

"You may as well pull everything out. For the inventory that the solicitor tells me will be necessary."

"Because she died intestate?" McGarr asked, reaching into the shadows of the safe.

"Aye. She had made no plans for her death."

Which meant that her entire estate would revert to her father. After taxes.

From one side of the safe, which was surprisingly deep, McGarr's hand came up with two stacks of sterling notes in fifty-pound denominations. He fanned them—fifty each, he guessed, which made five thousand pounds. All crisp notes. He reached in again, but otherwise the safe was empty. He handed the stacks to Nelson.

"That's all?" the older man asked.

McGarr bent his neck and looked in. "Yup."

"That's strange. I don't mean to seem grasping, but I know for a fact that Nellie hadn't made a deposit in at least six months. She spoke to me on the phone only a day before her death, said she'd been too busy, and she wished I lived a little closer so I could help her out with little things like that. 'Why don't you retire? You don't need to be running out at all hours of the night in bad weather after some gorsoon's sick calf. I've got money enough for both of us.' Her words."

McGarr stood and regarded the man, waiting for an explanation.

Plainly embarrassed, Nelson reached into his pocket and withdrew what looked like a bank deposit book. "I don't know how to word this nicely, but I'm afraid my Nellie was a bit of a thief. From the government. By that I mean, whatever money she took in from foreign sources, she kept. And did not report. You know, as income. As far as the government ever knew, her business was just scraping by.

"Every so often she'd drive over to Strabane in the North and put her profits in one of those 'blind' accounts for 'foreigners' they have there. Years ago when she spent all that time in Canada writing for magazines, she became a dual citizen. She got herself a passport and everything, which has proved useful. At the bank."

"But why in British pounds?" Noreen asked.

"It eliminated any questions about her deposits being in Irish pounds.

"But"—he opened the deposit book— "from what I can see here, she hadn't made a deposit in six...no, *nine* months. And the amounts were getting larger and larger, as the business improved. Would you care to look?" He held out the book.

McGarr moved toward it, at the same time handing Millar the stack of sterling notes.

As McGarr flipped through the pages, noting the sums, Nelson said to Noreen, by way of apologizing for his daughter, "Nellie always said she recognized no government but the government of nature. And then she claimed that the only advantage in owning a retail enterprise was the opportunity of taking tax-free profits. Given the long hours and having to please the public, as she did."

"Ah-men," replied Noreen, who in her own retail operation maintained two sets of books that one day— McGarr had observed more than once—might get her (and *them*) into trouble. But not as much as he might already be in. Back in Dublin.

Nellie's deposits in the North had begun some eight years earlier, most at regular quarterly intervals. Only once had she waited six months, and then the sum deposited was somewhat larger than for the six months of the preceding year. "This is a lot of money," McGarr said.

"Oh, it's the catalog business that was the real moneymaker. Have y'not seen the catalog?" Nelson turned to a stack of glossy, magazine-size booklets on the desk. He handed one to Noreen, another to McGarr.

"People are mad for mail-order shopping, especially in North America. And most items—the rods and reels and vests and parkas and the like—Nellie never even had to handle herself. She merely set up her 'line,' as she called it, and jobbed out the production of the items. She spent most of her time on the catalog itself, making sure it had the right 'look.' You know, for the people who could afford some of those things. The prices she got!"

McGarr again scanned the column, then flipped to the final page of numbers. During some quarters in recent years, the figure of some quarterly deposits was over 60,000 pounds, especially right before Christmas and in the late winter, when fishers began to reequip themselves for the coming season. And in all Nellie had squirreled away slightly over 700,000 pounds.

"And you say Nellie had not made a deposit for three quarters?"

"She said she had been busier than ever, what with the catalog stuff, the shop, and the fishing classes which there were more of. Also there was the Scottish woman, whose hand she had to hold, she told me."

"Niamh Goulding," McGarr supplied.

The older man nodded. "She was 'haunting' her, Nellie said. Wouldn't leave her alone, wanting to know this, that, and the other thing—about fishing, which she hadn't done much of, about the shop, about the catalog business."

"And Nellie told her?" Noreen asked, unabashedly peering over McGarr's shoulder at the final tally in the bank deposit book. "Oh, my word!"

"Nellie said she didn't mind. A little competition never hurt anybody, and then, if—but more likely *when*—the Scottish woman's operation on the Spey went down, she might make an offer for it herself. You know, by way of expansion."

McGarr's conception of Nellie, as entrepreneur, was changing. Hers had been no small, local concern. He tried to compute what nine months of foreign catalog sales might have brought in. If the business had been doing better than ever—say, 150,000 pounds. Conservatively, since he did not know how much better. His eyes darted to the volume of mail that was still stacked up by the door.

Motive enough for murder? McGarr rather thought so.

Noreen was flipping through the pages of the catalog. "I had no idea *Useful Silence* was Nellie's brainchild." It was a slip of the tongue, and she glanced at Nelson. He did not seem to have heard her. "I've been seeing it on my mother's coffee table for, oh—"

"Five years," Nelson supplied.

"I was always attracted by the name." Noreen glanced at

McGarr. "It's that line from Menander's essay about how life is little more than a farce, and often it's best to hold your tongue." Good advice for herself, she judged, since, after all, it was tragedy that had brought them together. But she rambled on, "The stuff in here is dear, no question about it. But it's first quality in everything."

Like the materials in the flies Nellie had made, thought McGarr. "Who else would have the combination to this safe?"

"Nobody that I know of. Nellie was ... Nellie. She fancied doing things herself, and she had the energy." As though suddenly lost, Nelson let his eyes roam the long shop. "Any success she had from this place, she earned and was hers."

"Not Hank Stearns's?" McGarr was thinking of the new sterling bank notes he had discovered in the Yank's billfold.

"*Especially* not Hank Stearns's. You saw what she wrote about Hank Stearns in her diary. Hank Stearns was an aging woman's ... fling, and nothing more."

"Who's Hank Stearns? Do I know him?" Noreen moved toward Maddie, who was trying to pull a net out of its slot in a cylindrical rack.

Said McGarr, "When I spoke with him, he called himself a partner in this operation."

Nelson's hand reached for the back of the desk chair, which he pulled out and sat in. Just in time, it seemed to McGarr. "That man can claim anything he wishes, and he might have *courted* the business. But it would change *all* that I ever knew of Nellie, if she had bestowed even a small percentage on that bastard."

"Well, I must certainly be brought up to speed on this matter, if I'm to be of any help," said Noreen, struggling with Maddie and the net.

McGarr had moved to the fly-tying table.

"What about the supply of jungle-cock? Could it have been exhausted?"

"Not in a lifetime—hers, mine, and yours combined. It was years ago when the stuff could be had for a pittance at its point of origin, and my friend brought back all he had room for in a large case."

"Then where would it be, if not the safe?"

Nelson shook his head.

"The house?"

"Could be, but Nellie would sooner lose the shop than the house. She loved the house, and she kept it open. The jungle cock has got to be around here somewhere." His eyes roamed the shop.

"Would Nellie have tied so many incomplete Jock Scots?"

Nelson shook his head. "It wasn't like her. Or, at least, how I taught her. The point is to complete each fly, so, if you're tying incorrectly, the mistake will be seen in the finished fly, and not be replicated in others. The jungle cock is here someplace in the shop."

Again McGarr pondered what he was seeing. If her father—who knew so much else about his daughter and the shop—did not know where it was, certainly whoever (if not Nellie) had tied the incomplete Jock Scots had not either. What did he know about that person?

That person had possessed a set of keys to the shop, since there was no sign of forced entry, and the shop was locked when Nelson and Sergeant Treacy came down to look for a key to Nellie's new Land Rover, after she had been discovered drowned. The set of keys might possibly have been taken from Nellie's house, the front door of which Treacy had found partially open.

That person, wishing to impersonate Nellie in order to mask the time of her death and the theft of nine months of receipts, had put on a hat, similar to hers, and had sat at the fly-tying vise. Discovering an already tied Jock Scot either still in the vise or in the cork rail, that person began tying some others until he or she got to the end of the fly and could not find the jungle cock necessary to complete it. He or she tied a few more. Why?

Well, the other material for the "Scot" was already laid out. And perhaps that person believed nobody would notice the lapse.

McGarr tried to figure how long it would have taken him to tie the four incomplete flies. Hours. Say, three. He cut the time in half, since he was both an amateur and took his time, enjoying the process nearly as much as fishing itself. If that person had begun at one o'clock in the morning or thereabouts, it would have been almost daylight by the time he or she finished. In order to leave the shop without being seen by some pub crawler or fisher, going to or coming from the Owenea, that person would have had to wait by the door of the shop, step out, lock the two dead bolts, and steal away. Literally. With Nellie's money, after having taken her life.

McGarr turned to her father. "Now, think, Nelson—is there anyplace else she might have kept the jungle cock?"

After a while, Millar shook his head. "But I'll help you look, if you're of a mind."

"No need, I can—"

"No, no—it'll give me something to do. I don't fancy going back to the house."

But twenty minutes later, after seemingly having exhausted all possible places of concealment and found nothing, McGarr happened to glance out the window. Stearns's red Land Rover was still parked near the bridge. Sergeant Treacy was standing by the bonnet, squinting down at the number plate as he wrote up a summons. It gave McGarr an idea. "Hang on a minute—I'll be right back."

He found Hank Stearns and Niamh Goulding (he assumed) still sitting in the tiny lounge off the bar in Nancy's Pub, several empty glasses before them. Stearns was laughing volubly when McGarr stepped into the room, and he continued, as though to demonstrate to McGarr that his presence meant little to him. Finally he asked, "Help you, Peter?"

"Just what I was hoping. Would you happen to know where Nellie kept her supply of jungle cock? Her father would like to get it out of the shop for obvious reasons."

Stearns's eyes darted down to his glass, as though pausing to decide. He then stood. "Sure—why not?"

The woman's hand reached for Stearns's forearm, but he was already beyond her. "Hank? D'yeh really want to get involved?" she asked in a broad Scots accent.

"Hell—why not, honey? I wouldn't want the old boy to lose the place."

"I understand it's now a police matter," she went on, her concern obvious.

"Peter ain't the police, are you, Peter? Not anymore. He's just an old friend of the family. Nellie and him, hey"— Stearns raised his right arm, as though he would clap McGarr on the back, but he thought better of it? —"they went way back."

"Please yourself," she said. "I hope y'know what ye're about."

Back in the shop, Stearns moved straight to the bay window that looked out on the street. Reaching into the display of antique rods, reels, and fishing accessories, he removed an ancient wicker creel, which he opened. "Where better to keep something like this?" he explained, "but right out in the open where no conservationist do-gooder would suspect." He lifted the lid and pulled out a complete cape of jungle cock contained in a glassine sack. It was a magnificent array of gray feathers. He handed it to McGarr, then replaced the creel where it had been, making sure in a proprietary fashion that it sat on the narrow shelf properly.

Straightening up, Stearns staggered a bit, and his blue-green eyes shied past Nelson Millar. "Now, I don't know where she might have kept the balance of her supply. I know she had a bunch. But this is all she kept in the shop. Enough for the odd batch of flies." His eyes darted toward the fly-tying table at the other end of the long room. "Well, I'm off. Ma'am." He smiled at Noreen and touched the brim of his Stetson. "Nelson." He turned toward the door. "If you need any more help, Peter, just look me up. You're kinda good at that, ain'tcha?"

McGarr watched Stearns move across the street, not toward the pub but rather to his battered Rover, which he started up and drove off.

"I don't believe that in the course of my life I have ever despised a single person," Nelson Millar said. "Until now."

Going out the door, Noreen paused at one of the framed sententiae that were hung on the walls. She tapped the glass so the others would take note.

> *May your reel never snarl, the tip of your rod break, or you*
> *yourself return from a fishing trip dissatisfied with yourself.*
> *What a woman thinketh in her heart, so she is.*

"The top bit is O. W. Smith," Nelson said. "He was an American of a different sort from Stearns. Being a man of the cloth, he had a spiritual bent. The bottom line, of course, is the Bible."

Transliterated genderically.

# 12

# Culchie Freedom

Ruth Bresnahan believed that she now knew how POWs felt when, after a long captivity, they were finally freed. What war, you ask, could Ruth ever have experienced? Why, the BIG WAR—the ongoing, largely internecine, eternal war that will never submit to truce, peace, or amnesty.

"The bloody war between the effing sexes," she said to the windscreen of her self-consciously Yuppie BMW roadster, which she loved, as it impelled her over the South Kerry Mountains and into Limerick, Clare, Galway, Mayo, Sligo, and finally Donegal. The car was the one nice thing Ruth had done for herself since her father's death. He would have wanted her to have it.

Or a *long* captivity? Granted her rustication back in her native Kerry had only been nine months on the calendar, but to Ruth it had felt like an eternity that had seemed to blot from her memory feelings such as, "Freedom! Oh, *freedom*!" she sang, snapping her fingers to the cassette that she had by the sheerest coincidence slipped into the Blaupunkt tape player. God bless the technical superiority of the bloody Krauts, she thought. She could hear every tonsil wag, every fleck of spit that had struck those microphones in De-troit—no, no, *Mo*-town—dozens of years earlier.

The world she was now passing through was far different but filled with details not unlike those she was fleeing—farms, farmhouses, horses, chickens, pigs, cattle, dung—yet they never looked so bright and engaging. "Why, you ask—you miserable, Culchie wallies?" she asked out the open window. "Because it's *your* dung, *your* pigs, *your* cattle, *your* farms, and *your* stultifying, smothering, herd-minded, Culchie, wally friends and neighbors. Not mine!"

And she felt suddenly both ashamed of herself and—get this!—gladdened by her guilt at having condemned her past, her poor dead father, her doddering mother, her former fiancé, her many close friends, and about eighty percent of the country as a bunch of ignorant, benighted, tasteless, brutish, obtuse, agricultural sods.

As her good friend, Noreen McGarr, once pontificated when tight, "Social-cultural prejudice is the very best form of prejudice, since you can lacerate deserving targets, often to their faces, and they have no idea they're being sent up. It's something we learned from the Brits of course, but in matters of contempt—and its first cousin, hatred—we do them better."

Now on the wings of revulsion, Ruth's German chariot swung around the picturesque bend that was the southern approach to Ardara. Before her there was a stately house sitting under glorious, full-boled linden trees and looking out over a broad bay. McGarr's old Mini-Cooper was stopped in front of the door, where an older man was tugging himself out of the low vehicle. McGarr was at the wheel, Noreen and Maddie in back.

It must be the house of the murdered woman, Ruth thought, McGarr having filled her in on the phone when she rang him up to say she was coming. Yet she rolled on toward the hotel at the crossroads. Just to think that she was back on the job and undercover—a ruse she adored—gave her a high the like of which she had not felt in a dog's age. Well, at least a puppy's.

The crossroads, which was obviously the center of the small town, was crowded with tourists and packed with cars. Ruth thought she found a parking place when a battered red Land Rover cut in front of her, and a third car eased into the slot.

She had to wait nearly fifteen minutes for another space to free up, but it was opposite the Nesbitt Arms, where McGarr had advised her to stay. Toting her bag along with her father's encased fishing rod and a weatherproof fishing jacket, she stepped into the hotel.

At the front desk, which was a small, low affair just inside the door, Ruth discovered a middle-aged man who was busy perusing the sports columns of the *Donegal Democrat*, she could see. The front page, describing the funeral of Nellie Millar, was turned toward her.

When the man looked up, his eyes rose to the edge of the newspaper, to Ruth's narrow waist, up the smooth-fitting, black-striped-on-amethyst, cotton turtleneck jumper she was wearing, circled her definite shoulders and flame-red hair, and finally alighted on her slate-gray eyes. "Well—hallo-alloh-alloh-hah. That's Hawaiian for how do you do. Brilliantly, I can see. How in the name of every sweet thing may I help you?"

He closed the paper deliberately, and then regarded her

again with equal care. "By the way, I'm Cal McHugh, hotelier." He held out his hand, a sturdy man with a round face and an affable smile.

Ruth's hand was nearly the size of McHugh's, and she put her well-farm-exercised shoulder into her grip. "I'm searching for an accommodation."

"So wasn't Neville Chamberlain and look at the trouble he got into. I can see you're even carrying an umbrella." His eyes darted down on their hands. "I'll say uncle, if you will too. Ready—one, two, three."

"Uncle," they said together and released each other's hands.

"Whew! That was great! We should go on the stage," McHugh went on, spinning the register so Ruth could check in. "You're planning to do some fishing, I see."

"Yes," I thought I'd try my luck. Are the salmon running?" Ruth wrote her name and gave her Dublin address, which thankfully she had not abandoned.

"Even if they weren't, would I admit it? Not to you. How long shall I say you're staying for—is it, Ruth?"

Bresnahan nodded. "A week at least."

"Spot on. It just so happens that I have a room for a week at least. Let me tell you about the keys, before I forget. They're here." He swung open a gate beneath the desk. "When you go out, either hand the key to the lucky attendant or, finding nobody about, hang it up yourself. You can't imagine the keys we've lost over the years. The oceans, the mountains, the caves. The pubs." He winked. "Don't take this amiss, for I'm a married man, but do you know what Ruth means in English?"

Ruth studied McHugh's bald spot while he made a notation in his guest log. Looking up again, he said, "Pity and compassion. It's merely an observation, mind. We don't get many Ruths through here." He started out from behind the desk to take her bags. "More the compassion required."

Said Ruth, "I was hoping that I might get Nellie Millar to give me a few lessons. You know, fly-fishing."

That stopped McHugh. He straightened up from the bags. "I'm sorry to say that will be impossible." He handed Ruth the front page of the *Democrat*. "A wonderful woman, she'll be missed. But what I *can* tell you"—McHugh took up Ruth's cases again—"is that the salmon *are* running, scout's honor, and I'll see what I can do about getting you some lessons with some other experienced angler. We even have an American cowboy, of all creatures—a big, handsome galoot, by the looks of him—plying the waters of the Owenea at present. He catches fish, and I know he'd like you."

It was at that moment that the McGarrs pushed through the doors into the hotel.

Seeing Ruth, Maddie ran to her, shouting, "Rut'ie! Rut'ie!" her accent a near copy of McGarr's own.

Ruth reached down and picked Maddie up, swinging her around. "What a little cutie!"

"You know each other?" McHugh asked.

"I don't think we do," said Noreen, advancing with her hand raised. "We have a friend named Ruth who looks a bit like this woman, but not half so brilliant."

Introductions were made all around, and McHugh returned to porting Ruth's gear up a long flight of stairs, not seeing—Noreen hoped—her show Ruth the number on the key to their room. Or hear her say, "Come by in ten minutes. Peter will bring us up to speed."

"Rut'ie—aren't you coming with us? Where're you going, Rut'ie?" Maddie asked as Ruth followed McHugh up another flight.

"I'll be seeing you again, darlin'," said Ruthie. "Soon, I hope."

At the door to Ruth's room, which McHugh opened, he said, "Coincidences. Isn't life full of them? Only the other day I was saying to Nessa—she's my wife—that we haven't been seeing many Dubs lately. And here suddenly we got the best of them. Or the finest, as they say in New York of the lads and lassies in blue."

. "Do you know New York, Cal?" Ruth asked, looking around the comfortably furnished accommodation.

"Aye, a bit. Copper buttons, gold shields. Over here everything's silver, or is it tin?"

"I haven't a clue what you're referring to," Ruth said, closing the door. "I'd tip you, if you were anybody but the inquisitive owner."

"Ah, you already have, lassie. But worry not—I'm a rare man with inside information."

# 13

# Initial Reaction

Forty minutes later, McGarr rapped on the door of number 17, a corner room where the Scottish woman, Niamh Goulding, had been staying for nearly nine months.

"Come eee-in, the door is open," a woman's voice said.

McGarr found her seated across a large room by an open window that looked out on the square and was filled with brilliant light. There was a coffee cup on the ledge.

"Chief Superintendent McGehr," she said pleasantly, rising to offer her hand. "I've been expectin' ye. Henry should have introduced us, doon in the pub. But I reckon Henry is Henry, and there be no changin' tha'."

McGarr took the proffered hand. Niamh Goulding had changed into a cabled jumper with what looked like metallic threading that glimmered silver in the strong light. It had a wide, ballet neckline—McGarr believed it was called—that could be worn either on or off the shoulders.

Or shoulder, which was presently the case. One protruded nearly down to the elbow.

With the exception of the wedding band and diamond engagement ring, gone was the gold that McGarr had noted earlier in the pub. It had been replaced by silver and pearl earrings, a matching necklace, and a silver wristwatch with a silver band. She had even shadowed her eyes with a pearly brush.

From the waist down she was swathed in black slacks that were tighter—McGarr could not help but note, as she bent toward the ashtray on the window ledge to stub out her cigarette—than second skin. On her feet were black flats.

"Nigh, to what do I owe the pleasure of ye'r attention, surrh?" Sitting again, she fluffed her rich mane of honey-colored hair with a gesture that McGarr had seen screen stars employ. With her hands clasped around one knee, the wide neck of the jumper exposed one breast nearly to the nipple. There was a pair of eyeglasses draped over the arm of the chair.

McGarr sat opposite her on a low couch. "I'm interested in your recollection of the night that Nellie Millar died."

"Why, may I ask?"

"Because of the way she died."

Her tilted head swung to the other side, as if she were having trouble seeing him clearly. "And what way is that?"

As though having to think, McGarr let his eyes roam the room or, rather, the suite of rooms. There was a bedroom off the sitting room. Both looked as though they had just been made up; everything was neat and clean, and beneath the odor of her perfume and the smoke from her cigarette, McGarr could smell lemon wax. There was something shiny and out of place on an end table by the telephone— some sort of fat clasp knife. " 'Death by misadventure.' It's a term that begs definition, especially in Nellie's case."

"Since she was ye'r lover."

"She tell you that?"

"No—Henry did."

"And she told Henry, I suppose?"

"Wee-el, no. Having known Nellie, I do na' reckon she did."

At least that was accurate; Nellie had been nothing if not a private and discreet person.

"But that's Henry, isn't it. He's so visceral and . . . emotive, for want of another term."

"Like jealous? What would he have to be jealous about, having you, as I assume he does. You're the younger, handsomer woman."

Niamh Goulding's smile pouted her high cheeks. She had a single dimple and well-formed teeth, but McGarr could not get over the impression that her china-blue eyes appeared opaque and agatized. He wondered if she could see him at all.

"Why, thank you, Chief Superintendent, but certainly you didn't come here to discuss my sex life. With the emphasis very much on sex. With Henry." She reached for the coffee cup, and the exposed breast nearly spilled from the glittering jumper. The nipple was a tawny mocha color that seemed to belie her honey-colored hair.

"Would that be what Stearns had been about in the early hours of the morning that Nellie died?"

"Ye' know"—she pointed a finger at McGarr in a patently disingenuous fashion—"I believe it was. Let me recount my movements—is that how it's said?—on the night of Nellie's 'misadventure.' Perhaps knowing what *I* did will set ye'r mind to rest.

"Let's see." She leaned forward in the chair and placed her elbows on her knees. "It's really not something I've thought about much, and one day seems to flow into another here in Ardara without much change. Until recently, of course. Which should make that day memorable.

"Oh, yes. After fishing that afternoon, Henry and I had a bit of a session up here." A hand swung toward the bedroom. She smiled sweetly. "Nellie, you see, had arranged for him to be my actual *fishing* instructor some months ago, almost as though giving him to me. And, well, one thing just led to another, I'm happy to say. Henry is probably the major reason I've stayed on so long. Lamentably, they don't make men like Henry in Scotland anymore. Or in Ireland from what I can see, ye'rself excepted, surrh. Where was I?"

"The session."

"Right. Well, I'm a divorced woman." She glanced down at the immense diamond and considered it, twisting her hand from side to side, as though attempting to focus on it. "Actually, twice divorced. Successfully. And once widowed. Also, I'm not getting any younger, and I'm afraid I then fell asleep. Henry usually leaves me like that. I had planned to accompany Nellie and him fishing that night, since she had informed me that she expected a strong run of salmon into the Owenea. May I admit something?" Her china-blue eyes strayed in McGarr's general direction. "I'm desperately interested in every aspect of salmon fishing, but alas I've yet to land me first fish. Here in Ireland, that is.

"Any-hoo, when I awoke, I discovered that it was well after one. Nearly two. I forget what time exactly, but I felt refreshed. So I dressed and headed out, thinking that I might perhaps still fish the balance of the night and certainly the dawn, when, again Nellie had said, the salmon would be taking. With Nellie, you see, I'd placed my gear in Henry's Land Rover. It's that red banger you see about town. Even if he were fishing when I got there, I would still be able to fish, since he never locks the Rover. He can't. The locks are dashed.

"But"—she raised her shoulders and let them fall—"I no sooner got outside the hotel and to the bridge over the Owentocker here in town, than I saw Henry's machine parked there and a light on in Nellie's shop. I peered in and saw her at the back at her table. I figured Henry was in Nancy's where he usually puts in when he's caught a few fair fish, so I went into the Rover for my gear. My own car, you see, is parked in back of the hotel, and I thought I'd fish the dawn alone. Perhaps without so much ... attention I might get lucky.

"But the interior light in the Rover is shot, and didn't I snag my net on something and tear the meshing. I considered taking Henry's net, since once into the pub he usually stays." She paused, as if McGarr should take note. "But he's verra particular about his equipment, Henry is, and I thought better of it. Which was when I crossed over to Nellie's and tried to get her to come to the door. But rap as I might—and *did*—I could no' get her to stir from the table. She waved once, that's it, as though to say, Go 'way with yeh, I'm busy."

"Which is when you met Hal Shevlin," McGarr said.

Niamh Goulding eased herself back into the chair. Her cheeks pouted again, but the smile was brittle, her lips a perfect incarnadine line. "Aye—that I dee-id."

"You know him?"

She nodded. "To speak to. He's about the river most days. And nights, when the salmon are there."

"Fishing?"

"I wouldn't say tha' exactly."

"And you spoke to Shevlin?"

She nodded, and a shoulder reappeared through the

neckline of the sweater. "I suspect I complained that, after all the money I had lavished on the woman, she would no' even come to the door for me."

"And he?"

"Och—the same from him as always about Nellie. He called her a bloody bitch and more, and moved off."

"Off where."

She had to think. "Into town, I believe. That's right. He followed me back to Henry's Rover, where I began collecting my things. He asked me if I needed a hand. 'With anything.' Those were his verra words."

McGarr waited.

"I decided against fishing without a net. It would be just my luck to hook a good fish finally, only to find myself netless. I came back here and read for a while." She pointed to a stack of magazines, the top copy of which was an Orvis—the American outfitter—catalog of fishing gear. "Around six Henry knocked, and I let him in. But he was drunk, and I'd had enough of him the afternoon afore." She pulsed her depthless eyes at McGarr. "I hope I'm not shocking you, surrh. But a woman could easily lose her ... emphasis with a man like Hank." It was the first time she had used Stearns's moniker.

"How did you know it was Nellie at the tying table?"

"Who else would it have been?"

"She turned her face to you?"

"I dinno. She might've. I can't actually remember."

"Were you wearing your eyeglasses or contacts?"

She sighed. "Lamentably, I suffer from a radical astigmatism as well as myopia, and contacts are unsuitable. I've tried them. I must have had my glasses on. It was half-light then, and I would not have been able to move around without them. Or see Nellie from that hideous little display window she put up with in the front of the shop. That should be changed."

"By whom?"

"Oh"—she shook her head—"by whoever. Her father, should he choose to carry on. Or ... Nellie's successor?" She again smiled at McGarr.

"You tie flies yourself?"

"Yes. Expertly. It's something I picked up from one of my exes. It's how I got into fly-fishing. Contrarily, I'm learning."

"Did you ever tie flies in Nellie's shop?"

"Never. I offered, but she would let nobody touch her fly-tying things. Even during a lesson she would take out a Model A and clamp it to the end of the table by the office. And parcel out the feathers a quill at a time." By Model A, Goulding meant a Thompson Model A, a simple, cheap, but adequate vise that McGarr himself had learned to tie on and still used.

"But I required no lessons." There was evident pride in that.

"Can you tie a Jock Scot?"

"Of course." The answer was too quick, as though she had expected the question.

"As fair as Nellie's?"

"Indistinguishable. She tied an excellent fly."

"With excellent materials."

"With excellent, appropriate materials. She made no substitutions, and for that she should be commended. I'll do the same myself, or not tie at all."

"Even without jungle cock?"

"I'll find some, I'm sure."

"Why did you warn Stearns against helping me locate the jungle cock?"

"Because he was drunk, as usual. And in that condition, he's verra much like a child who do na' know what he's doing."

McGarr's eyes again scanned the neat room and fell on the object that he had seen when entering. It was a long clasp knife with a bright marlinspike folded along the side. He stood and moved toward it. "Like what?"

"Like whatever brings ye here. Ye'r 'misadventure.'" Her elbows moved up on the chair and the neckline of the jumper plunged. "I ask myself—could you be messing about with Nellie's death because you're suspended, and you just canna ken what else to do with yourself? Or could it be that ye're still in love with her, and you can't muster the gumption to deal with her death? Somebody must be guilty, somebody must be to blame. Maybe some—I don't know—some Billy Budd type, like Henry, who you obviously detest because he's so American—will do. D'ye hate *all* Americans? It's rather common, here in Ireland. Perhaps you should put *yourself* some questions, surrh, before you stir the pot and disrupt people's lives in this wee, tranquil village."

Her concern for Ardara, rather than her vehemence, intrigued McGarr. "What are your plans, now that Nellie is no longer here to—was it?—tutor you?" He picked up the knife and opened the blade.

"It was."

"Headed back to Scotland, are you? Where is it there? Exactly?"

She stood and grasped her elbows in a provocative way that wrapped the material of the jumper tight around her breasts. "Garmouth."

It was a harbor town at the mouth of the Spey, which McGarr had fished. He had passed several nights in Garmouth.

"But I haven't decided. It's all been so sudden. It's not just Nellie's death, it's the idea that I still don't know enough."

"To open a shop like hers, there in Garmouth?"

"The *shop* isn't the difficult part. It's acquiring the ... expertise, the reputation, the *élan*, if you will, to attract fly-fishers."

"What about a catalog? Are you planning one of those as well?" McGarr had to carry the knife to the window, where the light was better, to read the stamping on the butt of the blade.

"Why not? But there again, the trick is to get people to recognize and open your catalog. There's so much junk mail these days, especially in North America where there's an established mail-order market. And so many English-speaking people. Three hundred million on last count."

"But Nellie did well enough?"

"I'd hazard she dee-id."

Speaking of hazards, Niamh Goulding did not move for McGarr, and he had to squeeze by her. "Sorry."

"No, you aren't. Not one bit. But then I've always been aroused by men with spunk."

· Like Hank Stearns, McGarr thought. Men with spunk, who might be directed? It was a possibility. The blade said:

OFF SHORE
#440 SURGICAL STAINLESS
HARDENED TO ROCKWELL 57–58 SPECS
FLINT FORGE
FLINT, MICHIGAN

The stout, three-and-a-half-inch blade had been honed recently and was "surgically" sharp, McGarr judged. Just the thing that would cut through the thick material of a pair of waders with ease, he imagined. Yet the knife was not new.

The handle was checked and worn. Nor was it an angler's knife. With the marlinspike for working open difficult knots and a shackle opener, it was a yachting or shipboard tool. McGarr turned it over. Engraved on the stainless butt plate were the initials H.S.

"Where did this come from?"

"I don't know. I was about to ask the maid. I found it just now, when I returned from the funeral and the pub."

"H.S.—Henry Stearns?" McGarr asked. Or could it be Hal Shevlin?

"I don't know what ye're talking about."

McGarr showed her, but she had to resort to her eyeglasses in order to see the engraved initials. The two of them were now standing very close.

Niamh Goulding pulled off the glasses and flashed McGarr her wan smile, the one that pouted her cheeks and tightened brilliant lips. Up close, her eyes looked like dense blue buttons. "As I said, I have no idea. I never saw Henry with anything like that. Or, for that matter, with any knife. Henry never cleans the fish he catches. He either puts them back or sells them whole. And then, d'ye think he'd require a marlinspike for anything of that"—her fingers crimped the air—"bonny girth for angling?" Her eyes descended to McGarr's lips. "Fly knots are usually too small to be opened by such a . . . probe?"

McGarr carefully closed the blade, keeping the dividers in the handle upright so that the microscopic filaments of anything that might have been cut by it would not spill out. "One final question?"

She had inclined her head and was staring into his face. "Any wee thing."

"What's your definition of a 'successful' divorce?"

"One that leaves me smiling. Have ye ever considered the condition ye'rself? It must be dreadful, having to put on the same old shoe time after time. Och, but I forget—divorce is still forbidden to you Catholic Irishmen, isn't it? And must lead to much personal unhappiness."

McGarr discovered the chambermaid in a laundry room on the third floor. She had found the knife while Hoovering on the wall side of the bed in Niamh Goulding's bedroom. "I don't know how I could have missed it the first time."

McGarr waited.

"She came for me no more than a quarter hour ago, said that for all the kindness she's shown me I could at least do the carpet thoroughly. I got down on me hands and knees, and there it was."

The maid assumed it belonged to the "Missus or one of her friends."

"Missus who?"

"Goulding. She's a missus, y'know," said the maid, the perjoration plain in tone. "No husband about. Or no husband, more like it."

"Busy, is she?" McGarr asked.

"Aye, and then some. Night work, if you know what I mean. And plenty of it. Every so often, like this mornin', she gives me one of these." She showed McGarr a twenty-pound sterling bank note. "Hush money, I call it. I thought, when Miss Millar died, she'd be leavin' us, but Mr. McHugh tells me she's arranged to stay the month."

Down at the narrow reception desk, McGarr asked for a pen and paper. He then pushed through the leaded-glass doors into the dining room and took a table where he could watch the desk and whoever came and went.

Keeping half an eye on the door, he ordered coffee and wrote Hugh Ward in Dublin a long note, asking him to contact *Bord Iascaigh Mhara* and see if he could obtain all files and information they had on Hal Shevlin of Rossbeg. He also asked him to drop into *Eire Rod & Reel* to see if they had copies of all articles that Nellie might have written about drift-netting. "And reader responses, if any. The originals, if they have them."

As well, he informed Ward that he would be sending today by Garda messenger a clasp knife and a pair of waders, "for Tech Squad analysis." Could the one have cut the other, he meant. Finally he asked Ward to dispatch the fingerprint unit to Ardara to go over Nellie's fly shop. "Discretion is key. No uniforms, no Garda cars. Have them contact me first at the Nesbitt Arms." He added, "Ruthie has arrived."

He had only placed the note in the machine at the desk and dialed the fax number at the Serious Crimes Unit in Dublin, when Niamh Goulding came tripping down the stairs with a rod case in her hands. "Methinks I should make use of Henry, while I can," she explained. She was dressed in fishing garb with a handsome wooden creel slung over a shoulder. Its brass clasp had been polished bright.

After the door closed, Cal McHugh muttered, "If there's anything left to use."

"Poor man," said McGarr.

McHugh nodded. "Me heart bleeds for him, donkey's hindquarters that he is."

McGarr went back to the dining room and his coffee, and waited until McHugh left the desk. Then, pretending to check the fax machine for a reply, he reached over the desk and opened the gate where the room keys were kept.

With #17 in his pocket, he stole up the stairs.

# PART IV

When fishing for salmon, the choice of flies is
not science but an art.

—NELLIE MILLAR

# 14

# Chuckles

A half hour earlier, Ruth Bresnahan had arrived in Nancy's Pub. Wearing pleated white linen shorts over a black bodysuit with a squared neckline and princess seaming that made everything else look "neatly" exposed, she collected all eyes, especially when having to bend her head just to squeeze into the low barroom.

It was noisy and smoke-filled now in late afternoon of a high summer day, with tourists and many locals—she could tell from their distinctive Donegal burrs—who were celebrating a football victory in the Ulster Cup that would take Donegal to the All-Ireland match in a few weeks' time. The radio had been full of it on the drive up.

"Ballygowan spring water with ice," Ruth ordered. "I'm trying to watch my figure," she said to nobody in particular.

"A highly competitive field, I'm sure," said the bearded barman with a smile. "Would you care for a twist?"

"Of what?"

Another tall person, the barman blinked, then straightened up and looked out over the heads of his other patrons toward the little light that narrow windows at the front let into the tiny pub. He craned his head to one side, allowed a smile to spread over his handsome features; he began laughing, which continued as he tonged cubes into a glass. He added a twist of lime and poured Ruth's spring water.

Reaching it toward her, he said, "I have a little theory about Irish women. Care to hear it?"

She nodded and leaned forward.

Into her ear he said, "As to looks, the women of Ireland are for the most part either cows or queens. There is little middling ground. Every so often, however, a woman comes along who will stop your heart." As he raised himself up, his eyes flickered down into her bodice. He then sighed. "Now, my good woman, drink your Ballygowan in good health, knowing your mere presence may be the cause of cardiac arrest."

"Which is power," said one of the other men sitting near enough to have heard.

"Or killer good looks."

Some others began chuckling.

"Why, thank you," said Ruth, reaching the barman a pound coin in payment for the mineral water.

He raised a palm. "No—it's on me. My treat." He adjusted his belt and scanned the glasses of his other patrons.

"But it was worth a pound, hearing you say that."

"No, as I said, having you here is like a tonic." With a fist he thumped his chest, as though to start his heart. "It's great to be alive."

"Even at forty-something, Charles?"

"Well, me imagination is still rampant." More laughter

ensued, and he turned to his other custom.

Ruth sipped demurely from her glass, having noted that the last head at the bar to turn toward her was decked with a well-worn Stetson hat. It could only be the man, Hank Stearns, from the description McGarr had given of him. He had been speaking with two blond, obviously Nordic young women who were wearing hiking boots and had large knapsacks at the side of their table.

"Get a glimpse of what's underneath them musk-ox sweaters, Chazz, we might be surprised. But whew! Don't think either one of 'em's seen a bar a' soap since Narvik, wherever the hell that is? What's that on your kisser, honey—bear grease?"

The blonde in pigtails then translated what the cowboy had said to the other one, who had a pelt of fine blond hair on her tawny legs. They both looked at Stearns and laughed.

"You virst," Pigtails said. "Take off your hat zo ve can zee your horns."

"Fetch them another wash, Chuckles. 'Least that way we'll know what's inside is clean."

Which was acceptable to the two women; if he was buying, they were drinking. The hirsute one raised her pint glass to him, her light eyes merry; Ruth's guess was they were gay. "Skol, Hunk."

"You don't know that yet, do you, darlin'," said Stearns.

"But *we* do," muttered the barman, filling the additional pints. "Question is, hunk of what? *Chuckles*. What next?"

Stearns paid for the pints in British pounds, and there was some discussion about the exchange rate, with the humorous barman saying, "Hunk—I mean, Hank, I'm not a bank, which is up the street."

"Too far," said Stearns, waving the change to the bar.

It was delivered with a sharp slap and a "Thank you, Hank. My man!" The barman was obviously growing tired of Stearns but not his custom, which appeared to be significant. Who else but a gobshite such as he would buy a round of drinks for two women, who were probably gay and were obviously making sport of him? He had money to burn.

Still Ruth waited. Stearns's roving eye would eventually find her, and it would be better if he made first contact with her, Cal McHugh—the hotelier—having said he told Stearns about her.

Only moments later a voice said in her ear, "You must be Ruth." His breath was hot and laden with the reek of sweet whiskey.

Ruth had been sitting with her elbows on the bar, and she now turned to him.

His curiously colored eyes moved from her face, down her torso, her legs, and back up. Arrogantly. Appraisingly. He liked what he saw. "Cal mentioned you were a looker. I'll say one thing, he don't lie. I'm Hank Stearns. What *all* can I do for you?"

"*All?*" Ruth asked over the rim of her glass, making sure their eyes met. "He told me you're married."

"Cal say that? He, of all people, should know I'm not."

Because of many nights you spend gratis in his hotel, Ruth thought. She now took him in in an equally appraising fashion—slowly, deliberately—noting the wide shoulders, thin hips, and slightly bowed legs that the tight jeans and flared boots rather exaggerated. With the hat and the blond-fringed, shoebrush moustache, he looked like a younger version of the man in the Marlboro cigarette advert. It was a coldhearted, killer image, Bresnahan had always thought, the sort of man who would do you in without a second thought on the principle that only the *physically* strong should survive.

"Well, since you're not married," she now said, "why don't we start with fishing, which I'm equally eager to learn. I came here, you see, to engage the services of Nellie Millar. But—"

"My partner," Stearns cut in. "My *former* partner." He shook his head. "I handled the rod and stream techniques. Nellie was the fly-tying and equipment side of the operation. The catalog and all."

"But I'd also like to learn how to *tie* flies. My father"— she lowered her head —"who's recently passed away—he tied his own, and it was my intention—"

Stearns shook his head. "It's not necessary. I never learned myself. It only takes away from the time you can spend in a stream, and why bother, when you can get any fly you want tied for a dime apiece by some mestizos in Nicaragua. All you need to learn is how to read a stream—what's in it for fish to feed on, what's hatching at the day and hour you're fishing, what in your fly book approximates the appearance of that hatch, and how to present it in a natural way. In fact, you get something— anything—in front of a trout's snout and you play it right, he'll bite."

"Like in salmon fishing."

"You've salmon-fished before?"

"As I said, my father was an amateur fisherman."

Stearns regarded her again, and his odd eyes seemed to clear. "Didn't I see you earlier, driving into town in—was it?—a new white BMW?"

Ruth nodded. "You cut me off."

"How long you here for?"

She raised her shoulders and let them fall; his eyes plunged. "For as long as it takes. To learn fly-fishing, or

*173*

at least to get a good start. But with Nellie Millar—"

"Don't you work?"

"Well—I *did* work. In Dublin. But *why*, if it's not really necessary?"

"Chazz!" Stearns called, downing the whiskey in his glass and reaching past her to set the glass on the bar. "Fix us up over here, will ya?

"Like I said, don't worry about Nellie having passed away," he confided into her ear as he straightened up. "Before you leave Ardara, I'll give you all you need...to know how to fly-fish." And more, his eyes said.

"What about you, Niamh?" the barman asked somebody immediately behind them. "Would you care for anything yourself?"

"Niamh, baby," Stearns said, pivoting to wrap an arm around a woman in back of them. "You know what I got here? Our first client. This here is Ruth. She came all the way out from Dublin for Nellie. I was just telling her how you and I could combine our talents and get her started fly-fishing."

Niamh Goulding fitted on the spectacles that were dangling from her neck and examined Ruth, who felt like a bug under the bead of twin magnifying glasses.

"My father just died," she said again. "He was a fly-fisherman, and he was always after me to learn. I thought as an...homage to him, I'd carry on with the sport."

"Cal McHugh sent her our way," Stearns put in rather defensively. "I figure I teach her streamside, you get her going with the flies."

When the woman removed her eyeglasses, a thin smile spread across her pretty features. "Of course—is it Ruth?" She extended her hand. "I'm verra pleased to meet you, I'm sure."

"Two questions," Ruth said, if only to make everything

seem legitimate. "What are your charges, and when do we start?"

"Oh—we'll charge, what?" Stearns had to think.

"What Nellie charged, certainly," Goulding said, the smile still wrinkling the corners of her eyes; she was a woman only a few years older than Ruth herself. And capable, that much was plain.

"But Nellie was the famous Nellie Millar."

"Who could not fish half as well as you, or tie half as well as I. It's a hundred pounds per day plus expenses, my dear. Henry is also a stream entomologist, a graduate scientist whose specialty is the animal life that inhabits streams, rivers, and lakes. Pee, haitch, dee. He is far more knowledgeable of the *science* of catching trout and salmon than Nellie, who thought of it as an art.

"I know it sounds like a great deal of money," Niamh Goulding went on affably, touching Ruth's wrist with three fingers. "But in a year or two our Henry here will be better known by *men* as well as women fishers than Nellie—great, good woman that she was. Rest her soul."

"Really?" Ruth asked innocently. "How will he manage that?"

Glancing up at Stearns proudly and almost—was it?—in a motherly way, Goulding said, "Why—somebody will have to take up Nellie's slack and contribute to the magazines that kept her name at the forefront of the sport. And then, with Henry's scientific perspective, his articles won't be the same old Nellie Millar pap—ye know, in love with the trees, the rocks, the wind, and the sky. He'll concentrate on the fish and the bloody water."

Exactly, thought Ruth.

"Have y'finished the article on her death yet, Henry? Or air ye still in mourning?" A long, silver fingernail rang off the lip of Stearns's glass.

He only looked away.

"And what's ye'r other question, my dear?" Goulding asked Ruth.

"When can we start? I'd like to begin as soon as possible, before my...resolve wilts." She flashed a conspiratorial smile at Stearns.

"Why not now?" said Goulding. "Henry and I were just about to venture out to the Owenea to give *me* a lesson. You could accompany us," and I can keep an eye on you two, went unsaid.

"Oop—did I say we were going fishing this after'?" Stearns asked, reaching for his fresh glass. "It must have slipped my mind. I got a little something I gotta take care of."

"Like what?"

"Like something personal."

With the smile still tightening the lineaments of her face, Niamh Goulding asked, "What possibly could you have to do of a personal nature that would not involve me?"

Stearns shook his head. "I don't want to go into it."

"Y'mean, with Jane and the children?"

Stearns's brow furrowed. "If I told you once..."

"Oh, don't be juvenile, Henry—d'ye think by not speaking of them they'll simply go away. Ye're going to have to deal with the problem, especially if we're to go on here."

Stearns drank off the glass in a swallow. "Niamh, honey—can I say something to you. *We* might be partners"—he glanced at Bresnahan and added—"buddies, pals, goombahs—the works. But like we agreed a few days ago"—he wiped the whiskey from his moustache—"you don't question me, I don't question you. Got that?" He waited, his deeply weathered features set, until she nodded.

"How 'bout a little later?" he said to Ruth. "We can go

over your ... equipment, maybe practice a few casts, and get a jump on the morning. You're at the hotel, right?"

"Yes, but couldn't I get started on *something*? Buying some gear or tying?" She glanced at Niamh Goulding.

"See you later then, Ruth." Stearns squeezed her shoulder and turned to make his way through the crowd.

Goulding waited only until he had rounded the corner into the hall. "Henry mentioned fresh starts, which I verra much prefer, don't you, Ruth? A new day for the fly dressing—say, Monday or Tuesday of the coming week, after you've used some flies and know what they're about." She did not wait for a reply, but turned and followed Stearns outside.

Watching from a distance a short while later, Ruth saw her confront Stearns as he was climbing into his Land Rover. Finally Stearns put a hand on her chest and pushed her away in order to close the door.

After he drove off, Niamh Goulding turned her face in Ruth's direction. Gone was her smile, and the expression that replaced it was ... murderous. Or so Ruth thought, though admittedly she was rusty.

# 15

## Assets

Not so Peter McGarr, who was in Niamh Goulding's suite at the Nesbitt Arms Hotel. He had scoured so many rooms in his time that no nine-month hiatus would serve to blunt his skill.

Niamh Goulding was a great woman for clothing and had packed the armoire, the dressers, and closet with every sort of apparel. There were dresses, shoes, slacks, shorts, blouses, bodysuits, leotards, jumpers in every color imaginable, also hosiery, stockings, underwear, and nightwear.

She was an even greater woman for that, with chemises, camisoles, garters and belts, merry widows, sequined masks, and a host of other trappings and scantily cut bits of lace that McGarr could not name. Some of those items had never been worn, and still carried price and quality-control tags.

Most of the new things had been purchased in Aberdeen and Belfast, but the prices of several items were expressed in dollars. He examined the labels:

## Assets

### Kaufman's Women's Boutique
PITTSBURGH, CLEVELAND, COLUMBUS, YOUNGSTOWN, WARREN

McGarr glanced up. Could Hank Stearns and Niamh Goulding have known each other *before* Stearns met Nellie and pursued her, as Nellie's father would have it? Perhaps Goulding had only accompanied him back to the States, when he returned to visit his nonwife and children. How old could the youngest child be? A tiny baby, say, four months. Add nine. Thirteen months ago Stearns had been acceptable enough to the nonwife, Jane Trowbridge, to have had sex with her.

Stearns had not yet arrived in Ireland, though he might well have already met Nellie and followed her to Patagonia and other fishing venues, as her father had said, which must have cost a fair amount of money. In spite of a good salary and his wife's income, McGarr himself did not have the kind of money to travel to the southern tip of South America, to say nothing of the expenses of actually getting to and fishing the wild shores there. And even if Stearns had been writing articles for various sportfishing magazines free lance, what could that pay? Expenses of that magnitude? McGarr rather doubted it.

A drawer in the table by the bed revealed a number and variety of condoms—ribbed, tasseled, *flavored*?—that amazed McGarr. It was as if he were staring down into the stock of a chemist's shop in Dublin. But given the probable difficulty of obtaining such items in rural Donegal (and whatever gossip the attempt might generate), the contents of the drawer were doubtless necessary armor for the "sexually active," he believed the phrase was.

On the desk in the bedroom was a small, new, and obviously expensive laptop computer that was attached by a cable both to a telephone and to—McGarr had to pick up the machine and turn it over—a portable printer. He wished he knew more about computers, but alas the electronics revolution, which had swept the world, had left McGarr untouched. Truth was, he could not even touch-type.

In a desk drawer, however, he discovered a stack of articles, dating back six years, that Niamh Goulding had attempted to write on aspects of sportfishing for a number of periodicals in Ireland, the U.K., and the States. One, which had to do with a simpler method of attaching wings to the Spey Fly, had been published in the *Garmouth Times/ Herald*, a clip of which was attached to the computer printout. But the others were either still in manuscript form or stapled to rejection slips. McGarr scanned them.

Most were form letters, but some, while commending the prose of the piece, said in various phrases of circumlocution that they wished she had included more description of her actual fishing experiences—"the drama of the stream, the strike, and the kill"—than her "excellent descriptions of locale and fishing history." Another said, "Less on the fly, more on the *use* of the fly and the *results*. Tell us about the fish you actually caught with your 'Silver Doctor' variant." Yet another said they would consider publishing her piece if she would "flesh out the narrative." McGarr wondered if that might include mention of whatever night adventures Niamh Goulding might have had on her fishing rambles. Now *that* would be a new twist in, say, *Eire Rod & Reel*.

Among the notes on a pad in the top drawer was the line "Ring up A. McPhee *re* H. Shevlin & key, elect., gas." The phone number began with a prefix for Scotland. McGarr copied down the number.

Could Garmouth be where Shevlin had intended to go for work? Certainly the knife that the chambermaid had found beneath the bed was more a sailor's (or at least a marine fisher's) tool than an angler's. Also, he remembered Shevlin's wife, Breege, complaining about his being out all night and coming back to her with "no money and trouble on him." A knife, like that, was just the thing that would have readily sliced through Nellie's waders. And certainly Shevlin—by his own admission—had access to Stearns's open Rover where Nellie's gear had been laid out. It still bothered McGarr that Shevlin, who obviously needed money, would have returned Nellie's rod and reel that could have "netted" him several hundred—perhaps even five hundred—quid. Murderers always tried too hard to make themselves appear guiltless.

The suitcases that lined the walls beside the closet were pricey Wathnes and contained yet more clothes that had not yet been unpacked. A large zippered pouch inside one was also locked, but it yielded to one of the picks on McGarr's key ring. In it were five deposit books, all from different banks, as well as quarterly reports from a Scottish building society where, it appeared, Niamh Goulding had lodged the bulk of her . . . fortune. There was no other word for it.

She held shares in mutual funds of differing sorts—equities, bonds, funds tied to the performance of a group of stocks listed on the London Exchange, funds that invested in German, Japanese, and American companies. She owned a brace of individual bonds written on private companies, utilities, and public works projects, most in the U.K. but also in France, Belgium, and Luxembourg. The interest from the various financial instruments with the building society was being paid into a "Cash Management Fund" and had generated over 40,000 pounds in the current year. From her withdrawals, it appeared that she used that source for her expenses. The total amount of her holdings in the society was just over 600,000 pounds.

McGarr scanned the deposit books, especially that for the Ulster Bank, which was the only Irish-based financial institution that she was involved with. The balance in that account was slightly over a quarter-million pounds. In a leather document case with her passport he discovered nearly five thousand pounds sterling in crisp, fifty-pound notes. Straightening up to glance out the window toward Nancy's Pub, McGarr thought of Niamh Goulding's definition of a "successful divorce" and if what he was seeing before him had been what had made her smile.

Plainly he did not know enough about her either. Her passport said she had indeed been in the United States beginning fifteen months ago. She had been issued a three-month visitor visa and had left on the day that it expired. McGarr replaced everything and locked the pouch.

At the bedroom window he now saw her leaving Nancy's Pub, seemingly following Hank Stearns toward his Rover, which was still parked on the bridge. Stearns pulled the summons from under the wiper blade and scaled it off the bridge into the Owentocker, before climbing into the truck.

McGarr moved into the sitting room and conducted a quick search that resulted in only one intriguing set of facts. In the magazine rack near the armchair, where he had found Niamh Goulding sitting an hour earlier, were a number of brochures with photos and descriptions of houses and property for sale in and around Ardara.

There was also a valuer's estimate of the market price of "Leixlip," South End, Ardara, which was Nellie's house, and "The Fly Shop Building, Riverside, Ardara." The note in bold type said, "Both values can only be approximations based on auction prices of similar properties in the area, since, at the client's request, the appraiser did not make contact with the owner or examine the structures in detail." The house was valued at 100,000 pounds, the fly shop "(structure not business)" at 50,000.

In addition to the several Hardy fishing rods that were stored in the closet in the sitting room, there were two Wathne tackle boxes. The first contained multiple reels, spools of differing-weight and -taper lines, and a number of fly "books" that were filled with a rather complete inventory of trout and salmon flies, all well made but little used. In that regard, both the second box and its contents were different. Filled with a vise, a strong table light, and all the necessary tools and impedimenta of fly-tying, the case itself was well worn and had not been packed with the care of the other. It was a jumble of items, much like the tying table down in Nellie's.

Returning to the first box, McGarr flicked through Niamh Goulding's dressed flies until he came to the Jock Scots. He removed one, which he wrapped carefully in his handkerchief and slipped in the breast pocket of his suit coat. He replaced everything as he had found it, left the suite of rooms, and locked the door behind him.

At Leixlip five minutes later, he found Nelson Millar sitting at the kitchen table writing out thank-you cards to the many who had sent flowers to Nellie's wake and funeral. "It gives me something to do. How's it coming?" Nelson meant McGarr's investigation.

McGarr poured himself a cup of coffee from the automatic pot on the counter and sat opposite his old friend. "Tell me, had Nellie ever thought of selling out—the house, the business—and moving away?"

Millar's ears pulled back. "Not likely. As I told you, after struggling for the first few years, she had only just got the business going, which was improving by the day. And as for leaving Ardara, it—*this*—was her home now. I don't think she would ever have left, apart from some extended fishing tour to someplace inviting. And who would have blamed her? She had made a wonderful life for herself here." Dressed immaculately in shirt and tie, as usual, Millar looked away.

"What will you do with the house and fly shop now?"

"Curious you should mention that. Before you walked in, I had a man here who made me an offer for the entire lot. Or, rather, a licensed valuer and real estate broker who made me an offer in the name of a client. He was plain about that." Millar handed McGarr the card of the very same valuer whom Niamh Goulding had hired to estimate the market price of Nellie's property. One Luke Bohanon by name, from Letterkenny.

"And?"

"We discussed the offer, and, when I could tell he wasn't prepared to go any higher, I told him I prefer to go to auction. He then asked if I had engaged an auctioneer yet, and when I told him no, he said he could also do that for me. But I'd sooner get a local to handle it."

"So you've decided to sell?"

Millar nodded. "As we discussed, the business, while brilliant, isn't for me. I'm too old, and, sure, there're only so many fish you can catch in a day. With what Nellie has left me and whatever I'll get for the properties—" He shook his head. "It's that everything's happening so fast."

"Does that bother you?"

Millar had to think. "Not in regard to the places—the house, the shop. The sooner I leave here and the . . . memories the better. But it's the . . . finality of it all, if you know what I mean, Peter?"

McGarr nodded. "I can imagine. What about advertising in some of the fishing journals, foreign and domestic, and selling the shop and business as a unit?"

"That passed my mind. Do you think I'd get a better price?"

"Possibly. Maybe one of Nellie's competitors would pay you a premium to take over the catalog. But you know, I've also been thinking of a way of offering the properties that might not eliminate the possibility of selling the business to a larger potential group of purchasers. Later."

"I don't understand."

It took McGarr a few minutes to tell Millar about his interview with Niamh Goulding and what he had later discovered in her rooms at the Nesbitt Arms. He then outlined the scenario he envisioned for the auction. "To be safe, you could name as the opening bid the price that you hoped to get for the properties and business. If nobody bites, you can always sell them at some later auction or in some other way."

"But when would it happen?"

McGarr thought for a moment. Speed was always important when breaking a murder case, since memories were fresh and time only gave a murderer more chance to cover up. It was now Monday. "Sometime near the end of the week?"

Millar thought again for some time, turning the pen in his hands around and around. The clip on the cap pictured a leaping salmon. "I don't see what there is to lose, provided I can arrive at a fair opening bid." He glanced up at McGarr. "And if you're convinced that somebody actually 'worked,' I believe you said, Nellie's death."

McGarr nodded. "I'm convinced of it."

"And we have a chance of catching them?"

McGarr nodded again. "No promises. But I think an auction might help, at least to understand who's ... interested. And if that interested party turns out to be the murderer, no court in the land will recognize the sale."

"So, you think it's the woman. The Scot. Niamh Goulding?"

"I don't know what to think. But we need . . . bait."

Millar looked away, and a thin smile broke slowly over his smooth features. "Sort of like fishing."

"Exactly," said McGarr, standing.

"Where're you off to now?"

"I thought I'd drive down to Killybegs and purchase a knife before the shops close." Killybegs was a fishing and shipping center a dozen or so miles to the south.

"What sort of knife? This house is filled with knives, and, if not to your liking, there's always the fly shop."

McGarr shook his head and described the knife he had discovered under Niamh Goulding's bed and had sent to Dublin for analysis.

"A sailor's topside knife," Millar said. "I've seen them. Handy things in a pinch, and the sharper the better. To slice a knotted hawser or tangled net."

"Like to come along with me? Maybe a few hours away will do you good."

"Just the thing I need. An airing. And I want to do everything I can to help."

# 16

## Little Leaps

The beach at Narin is one of the finest in Ireland and perfect for young children. A pristine sweep of tan sand sometimes hundreds of yards broad when the tide is out, it stretches for two miles along the shallow shore of Gweebarra Bay. People swim, sunbathe, and sailboard at Narin; others play football, rounders, or jog on the hard-packed sand of its tidefall verge.

Sometimes bathers think they can wade to Inishkeel, the small island that can be seen about a mile distant across the turquoise sand shallows. The beach declines so gradually into the ocean that Noreen and Maddie walked for perhaps fifty yards before Maddie was deep enough to "swim" with her feet still touching the bottom.

Also, the water was nothing like the frigid Irish Sea, in which they swam while in Dublin; here warm currents off the Gulf Stream combined with a full sun made the water feel almost tepid. Gentle waves, broken by the rocks of Inishkeel, sometimes lapped over Maddie's shoulders, but

Noreen did not feel as though she had to watch her every moment. Thus they passed a pleasant hour or so splashing and chasing each other, until the inevitable Donegal shower blew in over the mountain to the south.

It came on first as a mere glowering of the sky, with the sun still shining through a veil of cloud. But when the wind picked up, Noreen began the process of convincing Maddie that they should seek out the warmth and shelter of the car. Like most of the other bathers, she had driven it right down onto the beach.

The option was to remain submerged to the nostrils in the water, since the windblown rain, sweeping down off the mountain, would be icy cold but would pass quickly. Several of the older children, accompanied by a grown brother or father, chose that course, but Noreen and Maddie beat a hasty retreat to the warmth of their Jaguar sedan, which was a hand-me-down from Noreen's well-off parents and had been heating up in the summer sun for much of the afternoon.

They had only just made its toasty interior, when the sky suddenly assumed the color of dense steel wool, and fat drops of rain tattooed the car. The wind rocked them and howled around the windows. Noreen snugged a towel around Maddie and assured her for the umpteenth time that they did not have to go back to the hotel, and the sun would soon be out, and they'd be back in the water in no time. "Here—we'll have the lunch that the kitchen prepared for us."

"In the car? But I wanted a picnic! On the beach!"

Noreen sometimes wondered if they were spoiling Maddie, who was an only child. But her own parents had indulged her and her brother's every whim, and look how they turned out—two eccentric, self-centered-but-well-meaning people who were quite able to take care of themselves in the little that was left of the rarified world of the Protestant Irish Ascendancy. Everything that Noreen read in newspapers or was brought home by her husband, who was a sort of working-class hero, told her that Maddie's rearing could be worse, and she saw no reason to change her approach. But over Maddie's continuing objections, she now broke out sandwiches, fruit, juice, and a thermos of tea that she had only just poured, when she noticed the unfortunate woman down on the beach.

They had spoken to her earlier about a jellyfish that her children and Maddie had discovered beached in the sand. They were poking at it with their toes, and Noreen had rushed over, fearful that it might be a stinging variety that had been carried in by the tide from the warm waters offshore.

"No—it's a simple medusa," said the tall, gaunt woman, who was carrying a small infant in her arms and whose two other children, Noreen supposed, were gathered with Maddie around the transparent, purple-veined mass.

"Medusa," Noreen mouthed, staring down at the quivering disk. Her mind flooded with mythological reference—the story of the once beautiful goddess who offended Athena and was turned into a hag so hideous to behold that her visage turned all viewers to stone.

"It's the free-swimming stage of most marine coelenterates, by which I mean—"

"Hollow intestine," said Noreen. "In Greek."

"You got it." The woman's accent was decidedly American, and Noreen thought how wonderful it was that two people from two such different places could look upon one thing and think two such antipodal sets of thoughts, although there was the name. Somewhere, sometime, some classically educated sailor or naturalist had considered that primordial lump of living slime and thought of Medusa, combining close observation with the resonance of myth. It was the kind of little leap-of-the-intellect which, when coupled with all other little leaps, made up the mortar of civilization, Noreen believed.

"Jellyfish are invertebrates, of course, and are closely related to the hydras, coral polyps, and sea anemones. They also have both polyp and hydroid stages, but, like this, they survive by clutching small animals with their tentacles or disabling them with stinging cells. But this one is harmless, especially like this. Dead."

"How can you tell it's dead, Ma?" her oldest child, a sturdy towhead a bit older than Maddie, asked.

"By the opaque glaze on the outer membrane. If it were alive, Henry, it would be shiny and slick, but a fish, such as this, doesn't live very long out of the water."

As the children continued to question the woman, Noreen regarded her. She was not much, if at all, older than Noreen, and yet because of her gauntness and her ill-fitting cardigan and loose cotton dress, they seemed a decade apart. Perhaps it was the lack of any sort of makeup or the fact that she had a bony face and thin, if broad, shoulders. In all, but she was one of those rare women who would appear better with ten more pounds. Or twenty.

And yet her children, while also garbed in what looked like secondhand clothes, looked healthy and seemed happy enough. Noreen exchanged pleasantries with her and chucked the baby under the chin. "What's your name?"

"Diarmuid," said the mother.

"Are you Irish?"

"No—I just like the name."

Now, from the comfort of the Jaguar, Noreen saw the woman huddled by the water as the shower swept up the beach. She had to turn her back to the blast, the infant tucked under her cardigan; her other two children were lying in the sand shallows not far from her, trying to keep themselves submerged without being washed ashore by the now windblown waves.

"C'mon, Maddie," Noreen said. "We've got a bit of a rescue to perform. Let's spread the towels out on the backseat," which they did. Noreen then started the large, comfortable car and rolled down to where the woman was cowering from the blast.

Powering down the electric window, Noreen was pelted with rain. "Would you care to get in?" she had to shout.

"Well—I don't think so. It'll pass over soon."

"But more comfortably in here."

Still the woman hesitated.

"I have hot tea, sandwiches, juice, fruit, and plenty to go round."

The children bolted from the water, and the woman could only follow. Once inside, she said, "Really—look, we're getting your lovely car all wet and sandy."

"Nonsense. There're towels down, and that's what a lovely car is for—use. I'm Noreen, and this is Maddie." She passed the sandwiches and a carton of orange juice over the seat. "Dig in."

"I'm Jane," the woman said through a mouthful of tomato sandwich.

Noreen handed her a thermos cup of hot tea. Only then did Noreen put together the name, the American accent, and the young family with what McGarr had told her about Henry "Hank" Stearns, and she rejoiced. What luck! But then Noreen did not believe that luck was simply chance. She held with Yeats and the old Irish faery stories that luck was always in some way ordained. "Are you on your holidays?" she asked, beginning her interview, as it were.

"No—actually we're counter-immigrants."

"Really, now. And tell me, how is that?" Glancing in the

rearview mirror, Noreen saw that a flush had risen to her own cheeks; she should have been a Guard. Undercover, of course. She simply doted on intrigue of every sort, which was always better firsthand, like this.

"Well, you know how this country, since the Famine, has been exporting its poor and disadvantaged to other places, like the States?"

Noreen nodded; not only its disadvantaged, but more recently the graduates of its several excellent universities who could find no suitable employment at home. In recent years up to thirty thousand persons a year had been forced to leave, and emigration was built into the government's estimates for its operating budgets.

"We're running counter to the flow. Or at least my husband is at present."

"More tea?" Turning to pour from the thermos, Noreen asked, "And what line of work is he in, may I ask?"

"He's a stream entomologist. Or at least he was when he was teaching at the university. But American universities are using the recession as an excuse to deny qualified young teachers and researchers tenure. Instead they fill out their staffs with adjuncts. You know what an adjunct is?"

"The lowest form of humanity," Noreen quipped, having heard the jest from an American professor at a party.

They laughed, and the woman's baby began cooing.

"That's right—willing to work for next to nothing and thereby denying a full-pay position to somebody else. Hank wasn't willing to do that, and, anyway, he couldn't have taught enough courses to live on the little adjuncts are paid. Now he's using his knowledge of streams and fresh water to create a sports-angling business. Or at least he's working on it."

"Here in Ireland?"

"Yes."

"By sports angling you mean ... with the flies and all?"
The woman nodded.

"I know there're a lot of fishermen in Ireland, but aren't most of the tin-of-worms variety? Are there that many sports anglers in the country?"

"That's just Hank's point. Nobody really knows about the fishing here, which is world class. By that I mean, none of the international freshwater fishing community. There's the salmon and sea trout, but there're also lakes up in the mountains around here with lunker trout that have *never* been fished. It's Hank's intention to bring Ireland to their notice. You know, to promote the place and act as guide."

"I don't mean to play devil's advocate, but hasn't it already been done? Didn't I just read about some famous sportswoman—a fly-fisher, she was—who died recently somewhere right here in Donegal?"

The woman nodded. "Nellie Millar. She's why my husband came here. She was the first one to provide the kind of services that would interest people who travel to fish. But she limited herself to women. Hank's idea is to attract those men who, when they think about fishing for Atlantic salmon, think about Norway or Greenland or Scotland. As I said, Ireland's been largely ignored when, in fact, the fishing here can be better than in those other places."

"Were it not for the poachers, I hear."

Jane Trowbridge nodded and helped one of her children drink from a carton of juice. "Hank hates them, and they're a problem all right. He contends there are fish enough for everybody, if Ireland can just get some enforcement of the laws that are already on the books."

"You mean, about drift-netting. Those monstrous things twenty and thirty miles long that take everything. I've read about that too. It's an ugly business."

"Decidedly. Hank's all for live and let live, but he wouldn't hesitate to turn in a drift-netter. If drift-netting is allowed to continue, soon there won't be any salmon or sea trout returning to Irish waters."

"But isn't the netting of salmon a tradition here in Donegal?"

"*Draft*-netting is. That's two men in a boat and one on shore with the end of a small net. Sometimes they do well and fill their small boat, but never enough to damage the species. Otherwise, there wouldn't be any left. It's been going on here since before recorded time."

"You sound very knowledgeable about all of this."

"I'm a trained biologist, but I can also tie flies. It'll be my contribution when Hank gets going. You can tie at your convenience and still take care of three children."

"What'll happen to the Millar woman's...endeavors, now that she's deceased?"

"I don't know. It's a problem, if somebody were to take over who had the same idea as Hank." Noreen watched Jane Trowbridge turn her head to look at the figure of Hank Stearns, who was now walking toward the car, one hand clutching the crown of his Stetson. "Even if Nellie's father decides to sell the place, I'm afraid we just don't have whatever price he'll put on the place. Here Hank is now."

"Is this your husband?"

"Here comes Daddy, Henry. We'd better clean up the mess we've made and thank Noreen and Maddie."

"He's a handsome man," Noreen said. "Aren't you afraid some cunning colleen will snatch him away?"

Jane Trowbridge shrugged. "The way I look at it— there's plenty of him to go around, and he's devoted to the children. And then, I suppose, he's got to do what he's got do. To make us a living."

It was then the door opened. "What the hell you doing in here?" Stearns demanded. "I been looking for you for an hour. All over Narin."

He had not, thought Noreen; as few as fifteen minutes ago they were in plain sight from the road.

"We didn't expect you'd be back so quickly from Strabane. Did you get my clothes?"

"Enough talk. Out. Out!"

Jane Trowbridge put a hand on Noreen's shoulder. "Thanks—I haven't had the chance to chat with another woman in months."

"Perhaps we'll meet again," said Noreen, wondering what Hank Stearns had been doing in Strabane, which was in Northern Ireland. Buying his wife clothes, which were now much cheaper here in the Republic?

As the Trowbridge-Stearnses were walking away from the car, Noreen slid down her window and heard, "D'you know who the hell that is? McGarr's wife."

"The cop?" Jane Trowbridge tried to look back.

Noreen was moved to say, But I didn't know who you were when we first met.

"That son of a bitch wants to deport me, I can tell."

Maybe, thought Noreen. And maybe not until after a long stay.

# 17

# A Perfect Net

At sundown when McGarr's Cooper topped the rise south of Rossbeg, he saw that Hal Shevlin's trawler was no longer docked by his house. "Maybe he just decided to take a wee cruise," McGarr said to Sergeant Treacy, whom he had brought along for "blocking," as it were. With Breege, the wife.

Treacy shook his head. "A tighter man I've never known. If he went out, it'd be to fish. Since he can't fish without losing the boat, he wouldn't waste the fuel. He's absconded."

Which was confirmed when they got to the bright blue door of the thatched cottage. In it was Breege Shevlin with arms folded, a pair of dark sunglasses wrapping her eyes. There was a bright bruise on her forehead, and her left cheek was puffy.

"Breege," Treacy said, tipping his hat. "We'd like a word with your husband."

"He's gone where you won't be able to deny him a livelihood."

"Garmouth?" McGarr asked. "Sure, he's not there yet, and I can make one call from that car, and they'll bring him back *without* the boat." He pointed to his Cooper and the second aerial that was attached to the lid of the boot.

The short, dark woman, who was wearing a bib apron, lowered her arms. "You wouldn't."

McGarr said nothing.

"You'd as well take the house too. And the children," who could be heard playing at the end of the hall. Through the translucent glass of the door to the sitting room, McGarr caught sight of the reddish glow of the devotional shrine on the mantel.

Still McGarr said nothing. Behind the cottage to the west, the sunset was now a riot of blazing pink clouds.

"What is it you want? Maybe I can help you." She stepped out of the house and closed the door behind her.

McGarr showed her the knife that he had bought in Killybegs a few hours earlier. "Is this your husband's?"

She had to remove the sunglasses, and they saw that both eyes were blackened, the left nearly swollen shut. "It's *like* Hal's knife. But his is old and worn, and he etched his initials in it, so none of the yokes who worked for him would walk off with it."

"What would it have been doing under a bed at the Nesbitt Arms Hotel?"

"This? Are yeh *deaf*, man? I'm only after tellin' yeh—"

"What would *your husband's* knife have been doing under a bed at the Nesbitt Arms Hotel?"

She glanced back at the door of the house, as though wanting to flee inside. "Do you mean, you found the right one?"

McGarr nodded.

## Death on a Cold, Wild River

"Under the bed of the Scottish woman?"

"Niamh Goulding," Treacy prompted.

Tears popped from her injured eyes, and it was difficult not to feel sorry for her. True, she was a squat, dowdy housewife and no match for the lithe, fashionable, and wealthy Niamh Goulding, but nobody became a shrew by choice.

"Ah—I dunno. It's not been easy for Hal of late, as you know. Even as a lad, he was a bullhead, always wantin' everybody to do things his way, even if he was wrong. Like the whole world had to conform to him. When it wouldn't, he insisted, and he got fined and put out of work and nearly jailed. He went to pieces altogether. Staying away from here whole days at a time, comin' home with drink taken and sayin' how he was just tryin' to make a *connection*, he called it, like something off the telly.

"But *I* knew what he was about. Didn't I wash his clothes? I could smell the woman on him. But whenever I questioned him, I got the threat of this for an answer." She pointed to her face. "And, sure, I've more to worry about than who might be throwing a leg over him. Another child would be a disaster here, and we're good Catholics. Or at least *I* am.

"Anyway, after a while, he had some money for us, whether by poaching or whatever he was doing, and I shut me ears to what was being said in Ardara. And me mouth, until this moment."

"What were you hearing in Ardara?" Treacy asked.

"Ah, that he'd taken up with that bitch. The Scot, who's a divorced woman." As though the designation were an indictment, she let the phrase hang. "He was seen in this pub and that after hours, like happens here in summer." She glanced at Treacy. "Having drinks with her and the Yank sometimes. And leaving with her when the Yank—

who's got a feckin' family hi'self someplace up in the hills—wasn't about. But as I said, there was at least some money in it. For us."

Did she believe that her husband was trading *sex* with the Scottish woman for money? McGarr certainly did not. "When did he first show you money?"

"You mean, apart from the dribs and drabs from poaching? I don't know. A few days ago."

"*After* Nellie Millar died?"

She only regarded McGarr.

"How much?"

"A hundred quid. Sterling. Two crisp fifties. He had more, I saw when he handed it to me. But I don't touch his billfold. Not ever."

McGarr thought he knew why. "Did he give you the fifties the morning after Nellie Millar died?"

She eyed McGarr before answering. "As much as Hal hated that Millar woman and thought her the one who grassed on him, he wouldn't have killed her. He's a rough man, but not a murderer."

Nor a man who would have done anything to save her, by his own admission.

"But—" She nodded. "With having to pay the fine and all, we were down to nothing, not even much food. And with Hal being Hal—"

"No credit," said Shevlin.

"He'd burnt his bridges with most of the shopkeepers around here long ago, and I wasn't about to go a-begging to my family, who loathe him for this." Again she pointed to her beaten face.

"So his destination *is* Garmouth?"

She nodded. "He said he'd got a bit of a job taking care of some property up there in Scotland. I guessed whose property it was. But he said he'd paint the boat and put up some new numbers, if he could. And maybe after a while, when the Scottish authorities weren't looking, he might chance a bit of fishing. And with him gone my family might help.

"Here—" From a pocket of her apron she drew out an envelope. "Hal said, if you came back, I should give you this. I looked, I had to. I thought it might be a—"

Confession? But she said no more.

It was nearly dark now, and Treacy trained the beam of his pocket torch on the vellum of the envelope, which McGarr recognized as stationery that he had seen in the desk of the sitting room in Niamh Goulding's suite.

"I don't know what it means," she added.

The "Hal S." on the envelope had been crossed out. A ruled slip of cheaper paper inside said, "The net was perfect."

"What net?" the wife asked.

McGarr knew; Shevlin meant Niamh Goulding's net that she said she had ripped on the night of Nellie's death. The rip that Niamh Goulding said had caused her to rap on the door of Nellie's shop so she could get a new one. Which was where Shevlin said he met Goulding. At the door of Nellie's fly shop. "When did your husband lose his knife?"

"I didn't know that he had, and he'd never tell me."

Knowing you'd give out to him, McGarr thought. "What about fly-tying? Your husband ties his own, doesn't he?"

"I don't know what you're talking about. Come, I'll show you the extent of the man's angling."

In the very same closet in the sitting room from which her husband had taken Nellie's rod and reel on the day before, Breege Shevlin showed them as ugly a collection of razor-sharp barbs, spikes, and gaffs as McGarr had ever seen. He turned away in disgust and began leaving.

"Will you be calling the authorities about Hal?" she asked his back.

"Not unless I have to."

At the desk of the Nesbitt Arms, McGarr learned that an envelope, such as the one Breege Shevlin had given him, had been left there that morning for her husband. "That looks like the one," said Cal McHugh, "but it had a key in it."

"How did you know?"

"Easy. I could feel it through the envelope when Mrs. Goulding handed it to me."

"A key to her room upstairs?"

McHugh shook his head. "It was something like a latch key."

"She in?" McGarr meant Niamh Goulding.

McHugh opened the gate beneath the reception desk. Number 17 was hanging from its peg, which meant she was still out.

# 18

# Break(s)

Hugh Ward arrived in Ardara around noon two days later, feeling like a veritable teenager at his first dance. There he was, acting head of the Serious Crimes Unit of the national police, and he had not been able to keep his head from turning to every patch of red hair he had seen since he entered Donegal forty minutes earlier. And there were many here, where over the centuries the Vikings, while on their summer sailing holidays, had raped, pillaged, and plundered.

Ward was driving a Japanese car that he had rented at Aldershot Airport near Belfast early that morning. After collecting the information that McGarr had requested in Dublin, Ward had flown to Aberdeen, via Manchester, and hired a car there for the drive to Garmouth. Hal Shevlin's boat had not yet made port, and Ward had spent the intervening hours learning everything he could about Niamh (Fraser, Snipes) Goulding née MacHarris. He had visited the morgue of the *Garmouth Times/Herald*, the local tax office, and finally the Garmouth constabulary, where he presented his credentials and was treated with much courtesy.

He then watched Shevlin's blue boat (why paint a boat blue unless you did not want to be seen drift-netting illegally? he had thought) anchor in Garmouth harbor. After anchoring, Shevlin then rowed a skiff to the public dock with a large duffel bag in the bow. There he seemed to loiter in the shadows until it grew dark before hoisting the bag on his shoulder and carrying it toward one of the three properties that Niamh Goulding owned on the High Street in Garmouth.

At the door, he took a key from his pocket and opened it. When he bent for the duffel bag, Ward, who was now right behind him, shoved the short, wide man inside. There was a brief scuffle in the dark, but Ward had the advantage of surprise and much ring experience. Quickly he had Shevlin disabled, and the lights on in the foyer of the large townhouse that the Goulding woman, then Fraser, had taken title to in settlement of her first divorce.

"Don't bother getting up," said Ward. "Take everything out of your pockets and put it on the carpet."

"Who are you?" Shevlin asked.

Ward had identified himself.

"But you've no jurisdiction here. This is Scotland, not Ireland."

"You entered this country in an illegal boat. One call"— Ward pointed to the phone on a foyer table—"I can have it confiscated. For keeps, as I understand it. And the contents of the bag." It contained nothing but clothes.

Next they went back to the boat, where it took Ward nearly until dawn to go over it, stem to stern.

"Maybe if you tell me what you're looking for, I can help you find it," said Shevlin.

"About a hundred and forty thousand pounds sterling in fifty-pound notes," said Ward.

"Where in the name of sweet Jesus would you think I could get me hands on a pile like that? Tell me so next time I'll know." Ward kept searching, and suddenly a realization seemed to come to Shevlin. "You mean to tell me that the bitch had that much...loot in the fly shop?" He shook his head. "And there I'd thought I'd bust in and lift a few rods and reels. You know, in compensation for what she had done to me."

Ward knew for a fact that Nellie Millar had not been the one who had grassed on Shevlin. The letter that had been sent anonymously to *Bord Iascaigh Mhara*, describing Shevlin's illegal drift-netting operation at the mouth of Loughros More Bay, had been written on a computer and printed out on a portable printer. A Diconix, said the experts in the Technical Department of the Garda Siochana.

The very same printer had produced the several letters that had been mailed to *Eire Rod & Reel* denouncing the article that named Nellie Millar "the best fisher, bar none, in Ireland." On the other hand, Shevlin's submissions to that magazine—containing a strange poem about a hooked fish smothering when hauled from the water into the sickening air—had been penned by hand.

The photographs that accompanied the printed letter had been processed in Galway City, sent from an Ardara chemist's shop in the name of H. Stearns and picked up and paid for by him.

"What about the woman, Niamh Goulding?" Ward asked as he continued his search. "What's she to you?"

Shevlin hunched his broad shoulders. "A tumble. The wife—my wife—isn't much in that department anymore, and it wasn't as though I made the first move."

Or resisted much, Ward thought. "What about your

knife—the one with the marlinspike and shackle key. When
did you lose that?"

With an amazement that appeared genuine, Shevlin
said, "How d'you know about that? I lost it maybe six
weeks ago. No—two months now and some."

The inner sheath of the knife had contained fibers and
bits of rubber that were a perfect match with the material
of the waders Nellie Millar had been wearing on the night
that she died. "How often did you *tumble* with Niamh
Goulding?"

"Ah"—as though embarrassed, Shevlin looked away—
"whenever she was in the mood, I guess."

"How often was that? Beginning when?"

"Once a week, sometimes twice. She's the kind of woman
who needs a good man beside her. Nights. She told me
that herself."

It was always a mistake to credit your reviews, Ward
knew from experience, praise being the readiest hook of
all. Doubtless along with the *good* part. "Beginning?"

"I dunno. Beginning after I had my trouble."

"With the government."

Shevlin nodded.

"Where'd you get the readies you gave the wife? The
fifties, sterling."

"For feck's sake—she tell you about that too? Damn
her." He dashed a fist into the palm of the other hand. "It
was a loan. On account. Niamh wanted some work done
for her up here on her properties. I was desperate for cash,
and she advanced me some money."

"How much?"

"Four hundred quid."

"When?"

"A couple weeks ago."

## Death on a Cold, Wild River

Back on the dock in the early morning light, Shevlin asked, "What now? Are you going to take the boat too? Because, if you are, I'm going to try and stop you. Now."

"You'd better look at yourself in a mirror," Ward advised. "Your last attempt wasn't a roaring success."

But Shevlin moved in front of Ward as he made his way toward the rental car. "Really. I'm not coddin'. If you're to take me boat, you're going to have to kill me now. Because it's one and the same."

You should have thought of that before you took the boat away, Ward thought. "It's not for me to decide."

"Who then?"

"The Chief."

"What Chief? McGarr? He's no Chief."

"You're wrong there. He was absolved of all charges by the Tribunal yesterday afternoon. He'll be back at his desk in Dublin Castle next Monday." And thank you, Jasus, Ward had said under his breath; he had found the workload impossible without McGarr. Also, there was the idea that Ward had liked things the way they had been, *before* Ruthie's absconder. "Maybe if you stayed in the country more often, Mr. Shevlin, you'd know."

"Wait." Shevlin's hand was on Ward's arm. Ward looked down at it and sighed; he never enjoyed a punch-up out of the ring. He always ended up with knuckles too sore even to work the speed bag. "Can I tell you something? I broke your nose when we scuffled a while back." Next time it'll be your jaw, went unsaid.

"Could yeh put in a good word for me?"

"Like what?" Ward was thinking of the man's wife, McGarr and he having been in constant communication.

Next morning Ward caught the first plane out of Aberdeen.

# Break(s)

* * *

Now Ward had to drive the entire length of Ardara's main street, which was filled with obvious tourists, Irish people on their holidays, and locals celebrating the Donegal football victory. A flatbed lorry decked out in green and gold to resemble a stage had been set up opposite the Nesbitt Arms. A group of men were diddling with the wires of a P.A. system for some ceremony later on, Ward supposed.

Small white signs at various places also announced a PUBLIC AUCTION OF PREMISES. When Ward finally chanced on a parking place and got out, he read the fine print. It was the auction that McGarr had set up of Nellie Millar's properties: the house and the fly shop. It would be held at 6:00 that evening. Sealed bids would be accepted, if accompanied by letters of credit from Irish banks or recognized financial institutions. Only bidders could tender topping offers. The minimum prices were 90,000 pounds for the house, and 110,000 for the fly shop.

Ward found McGarr there. Yet another sign, saying INVENTORY IN PROGRESS, had been tacked to the door, but Ward, recognizing the unmarked Garda cars, walked right in.

"Sorry," said one of the Techies, rushing toward him to usher him out. "We're trying to get the place ready for the in— Oh, Hughie. I didn't recognize you without your ... togs." Ward was noted as a bit of a toff. "What's that you got on, a disguise?" Ward was wearing an Aran Isle fisherman's sweater and jeans. There were penny loafers on his feet; the lemon-yellow baseball-style cap on his head announced LAGUNA BEACH between twin palm trees.

McGarr was standing at a table that was strewn with feathers, staring down at a fishing fly clamped in a strange-looking barrel vise. They shook hands and conferred for a while, Ward telling McGarr what he had learned.

"Do me a favor," said McGarr. "Across the street there's a pub called Nancy's. Unless I miss my guess, you'll find Hank Stearns in there. Tell him you just arrived in Ardara to fish the Owenea. You thought you could purchase some flies at Nellie Millar's, but.... What you want are some—" McGarr then told Ward a number of names and a range of sizes. "We'll give you some equipment so you look authentic, in spite of your—" McGarr could not find the appropriate words for Ward's habiliments. "But, mind, you couldn't look more ... right."

Ward tried to read McGarr's face, but as usual it was impassive. "But how do I recognize him? Stearns."

"He's probably with Rut'ie," said McGarr.

Incentive enough. Five minutes later, carrying a forest-green leather case with red piping and a gold fish on the side and a similarly detailed tackle box, Ward eased his way down the narrow hall of the pub toward the bar.

The patch of red hair that he glimpsed there was *his* red hair—he'd know it anywhere—but Ruthie didn't even blink, seeing him.

Said the cowboy with her, "If what's in them cases is what I think, you're looking for me."

"I tried the fly shop. An old man there told me you could fix me up with some Half-Yellow and Blacks, some Thunder and Lightnings. I also need Lemon and Grays. And some Claret Jays."

"What sizes?"

"Four to fourteen."

"You need *all* those flies?"

"I lost my fly book on the Moy two days ago. We had a spill in the boat." It was what McGarr had told Ward to say.

"You know what somethin' like that'll cost? In these

211

parts flies are like twenty quid apiece."

"I didn't come all the way over here to hang out in a bar," Ward said in his best California tones.

"Lookin' at you, my man, I'd say you didn't," said Stearns, clapping the smaller Ward on the back. "But don't you worry, good buddy. I'll fix you up. Follow me. Be right back, darlin'." Stearns said to Ruth, who crinkled her eyes at him and puffed on the cigarette in her hand.

When did she start smoking? Ward wondered. She never smoked while she was with him. Categorically, since it was bad for endurance. Could Clint Eastwood here have turned her around? Had the cowboy gotten to her? He looked the type.

But as Stearns moved into the crowd, leading them out, Ward felt her fingers—he hoped—tweak his right buttock, as of old when she was *glad to see him*. When he twisted around to see if it was she, that great, glorious head of flame-red hair was tilted back on her tanned shoulders—bared courtesy of some floral princess-style bodysuit—and she was piping a jet of blue smoke at the ceiling.

At Stearns's Land Rover, which contained a wooden case of flies, Ward repeated his order and let Stearns choose the flies for him. "I've only just begun to fish. Actually."

"Hey—we all gotta start sometime," the cowboy said. "I don't want to push you, pal, but, you need a coupla lessons, I'm in town."

"Really?" Ward asked.

"Really, really, really," Stearns jibed. "You stayin' somewheres local?"

"I was hoping the hotel."

"Son," Stearns fixed Ward with his sea-green gaze, "I'll

see what I can do. The owner and me being pals."

Ward nodded, then paid the gobshite. He pretended to amble off toward the hotel, then returned to McGarr at the fly shop. With the flies. Saying to himself all the while, She pinched me arse. She pinched me bloody arse. Which gave him HOPE.

# 19

## Credit Scam

Noreen McGarr, being a gallery owner, loved auctions. And, given the short notice for the auction of Nellie Millar's house and fly shop, she was surprised at the turnout. By 6:10 a small crowd had gathered under the stately lindens at the side of Leixlip, but she suspected most were merely the "curious," for want of a more accurate term. Only a handful of envelopes had been delivered to the auctioneer.

Standing in the front row was Niamh Goulding, looking for all the world like a copy of the portraits of Nellie Millar that Noreen had seen in the house—brown, fedora-style fishing hat; khakis with a speckled, heather jumper over the blouse; butter-colored, half-rubber ankle boots. Slung from a shoulder was what appeared to be an antique wooden creel with gentle lines and a brass clasp that gleamed.

The color of the wood was a perfect match with the leather of the boots and, in fact, the highlights in her golden hair. From a gold chain hung a pair of gold-framed glasses which, hanging between, made her not inconsiderable breasts appear yet larger. She now put the glasses on to view another woman, who had just arrived and had stepped toward the auctioneer, handing him an envelope.

Noreen would not have recognized Jane Trowbridge, except for the infant that she was carrying wrapped in a royal blue shawl. She was wearing a wide, white sun hat with a blue brim, and a smart blue dress with white polka dots, Noreen first thought. But when Trowbridge stepped near, Noreen saw that the design was a small seal pattern that was a colophon print of a line of clothes offered by the upmarket Wathne catalog. What could something like that have cost? Five, six hundred pounds, Noreen guessed.

On Trowbridge's feet was an equally pricey pair of low-heeled shoes, also royal blue, that made her long, thin legs look almost shapely. Her stockings were white.

"Oh, it's you," said Niamh Goulding, when she recognized the taller woman. "Whatever are ye doin' here, woman? Where's Henry?"

"He asked me to look after our interests. I'm rather better at this sort of thing."

"What d'ye mean?"

"You'll soon see, I'm sure."

Bending to Maddie, Noreen moved them a step closer to the two women.

McGarr was seated with Nelson Millar, off to one side of the auctioneer, who now stood.

"Ladies and gentlemen, I thank you for coming here this evening. We're gathered to auction the stately residence behind me. I hope all of you have had a chance to inspect the premises and property and examine its many fine amenities.

"Also to be sold this evening is the business and premises of the deceased Miss Millar by the bridge over the Owentocker River in Ardara proper. Included in that sale is all inventory—a partial list of which I have here"—he waved a sheaf of papers—"as well as all other aspects of that business, including the catalog *Useful Silence*, and the right to continue those activities. A certified public accountant has examined the books of the fly shop and related activities and attests that it is debt-free." The auctioneer waved another sheet and placed the lot on the table before him.

"Are there any others who wish to bid on these properties at this time?" He held up a handful of envelopes. "No? Then I will open the bids in front of you now and announce the highest price on the residence first. If the figure of ninety thousand pounds is not met, the property will be withdrawn. If it is met or exceeded, I will announce the highest bid and accept any topping offers. Please remember that I can only accept topping offers from those who have tendered bids accompanied by letters of credit from a bank or other financial institution chartered in the Republic of Ireland or the Six Counties." He sat back down beside Nelson Millar and began opening the envelopes.

It was a curious auction, thought Noreen; the sealed bids assured that the minimum price would either be met or the auction would quickly break up with the least embarrassment to Nelson Millar. But then, too, it was a curious set of circumstances that had caused it to be held.

Noreen kept her eyes on the two women in front. Niamh Goulding could scarcely maintain her place. She was shifting her weight from foot to foot and turning around to scan the crowd, the thick spectacles confounding her otherwise sporting appearance, making her eyes look like twin dim blue orbs. Jane Trowbridge, on the other hand, seemed so calm that it was as though she had forgotten where she was altogether. She was rocking the baby, who was cradled in her arms, and singing to it in low tones.

The auctioneer stood. "Right, then. We have before us a bid from Niamh Goulding of ninety-two thousand pounds. Are there any other higher offers?"

"Ninety-three," said the voice of a man from the back of the crowd. He then identified himself, adding, "You have my bid and letter of credit somewhere there."

"Right. Ninety-three for Mr. John P. Gallagher of Bal- lyjamesduff." Who was a fishing companion of both Nelson Millar and McGarr.

"One hundred and one," said Niamh Goulding.

"Mr. Gallagher."

"One hundred and ten."

"And twelve," said Niamh Goulding.

"T'irteen."

"Fifteen."

The auctioneer waited. Finally, Gallagher said. "Six- teen."

"Twenty," Goulding responded immediately, as though completely prepared to go as high as it would take to secure the property.

"Mr. Gallagher, we have an offer of one hundred and twenty thousand pounds before us. Will you top it?"

"No, sorry—that's too rich for my blood."

Well said, Noreen thought—the property being paid for with blood money; she was thinking of the cash that had most probably been taken from the safe in the fly shop.

The Trowbridge woman kept crooning to her baby, oblivious to the goings-on.

"Whist now—will ye?" Niamh Goulding now said to her. "I canna hear."

"Going once to the woman in the front row. Twice." The auctioneer paused and surveyed the crowd yet again. "*Sold* to Niamh Goulding for the sum of one hundred and twenty thousand pounds Irish! Please see Mr. Millar's solicitor after the auction, Mrs. Goulding." He pointed to a man who was standing off from the others.

"Now for the business." Having already opened the envelopes, he held one sheet of paper up. "The minimum price has been met by two persons, the highest bid at one hundred and thirteen thousand pounds by one Miss Jane Trowbridge."

"What?" Niamh Goulding demanded. "Tha' canna be? She, *you*"—she turned on the taller woman—"don't have even enough to feed and clothe ye'r chill'er."

Jane Trowbridge merely kept rocking her infant.

"Have ye validated her credit?"

"I have it right here, drawn on the Ulster Bank, Strabane."

The Goulding woman's head went down, and her eyes searched the ground, as though pondering something.

"Do I hear any topping bids?"

From the back Noreen heard a man's voice that she recognized immediately, saying, "One twenty. I'm Hugh Ward, you have my bid and so forth in your hand, I believe."

"One thirty," said Jane Trowbridge, even before the auctioneer had found Ward's letter, which had to be ersatz. Ward had all he could do to pay for the loft he had bought on the quays in Dublin. Ward and McGarr were just drawing the Trowbridge woman out.

"One thirty-five."

"One thirty-five from Mr. Ward."

"One forty."

"One forty-five."

Said Niamh Goulding, snapping up her head: "One sixty, and we'll have an end to it."

Now the crowd was buzzing.

"I'm sorry, Mrs. Goulding," said the auctioneer. "The letter you have here lists an available credit of a quarter-million pounds, and you've spent one hundred twenty, which leaves but one thirty. That figure has already been exceeded by Miss Trowbridge."

"No—wait! I've more money." She flicked open the clasp on the wooden creel that was hanging from her shoulder, and pulled out what looked like bank deposit books. Noreen thought she also saw the glint of something shiny below. "I have it here. See?"

The auctioneer held out his hand, and she opened one book and showed him.

"That's surely enough, but the bank that the sum is lodged with is in Scotland, and we've no way of checking it at the moment. Under the terms of the auction, only Irish letters of credit are to be accepted. Unless, of course, Mr. Millar will accept your offer in good faith, and Miss Trowbridge will accede to the change in the terms of the sale."

Said Jane Trowbridge in an even tone of voice, "My offer is a hundred and forty-five thousand Irish pounds drawn on an Irish bank, and I have every intention of holding you and Mr. Millar to the terms of the auction. In a court of law, if I must."

"Then, I'm sorry," said the auctioneer, handing Goulding back her deposit book. "We have an offer of one forty-five from Miss Trowbridge. Do I hear more?"

Noreen saw her husband shake his head slightly, and Ward said no more.

"Right, then. At one forty-five, the fly shop and all its appurtenances are going to Miss Jane Trowbridge. Going once, going twice. *Sold* to Miss Trowbridge. Please see Mr. Millar's solicitor, and I thank you, ladies and gents, for joining me in the happy disposition of these fine properties."

But one party was not happy. Niamh Goulding seized Jane Trowbridge by the shoulder and tried to spin her around. "You ruddy, rude bitch—do ye know what ye've done?"

"And well," said Trowbridge, moving toward the solicitor.

"Where's ye'r husband?"

"I don't have a husband."

"Where *is* he?"

"Taking care of business, I imagine."

"Out on the Owenea?"

"He tells me he has a client."

"You mean—another woman to use."

"Whatever are you talking about—in *use* you have few equals, as I understand it."

Until this evening, Noreen concluded.

Niamh Goulding stuffed the deposit book back in the creel and turned toward the driveway.

"Could I see you for a moment, Mrs. Goulding?" the solicitor called after her.

But she did not seem to hear him.

Noreen saw McGarr glance at Ward and then nod to the Goulding woman. Ward waited a few moments and then followed in her train.

When Noreen and Maddie arrived at McGarr's side, he

was saying to Nelson Millar, "Could you come down to the shop and give me your expert opinion. There're three salmon flies I'd like you to see."

Turning to leave, Noreen could not find Jane Trowbridge anywhere among the crowd, but she heard the battered Land Rover crank over and start. Spewing a ball of diesel smoke up into the lindens, it passed out through the gates. Rather quickly, it seemed.

# 20

# On Style and Character

Down at the fly shop that might soon belong to Jane Trowbridge, McGarr asked Nelson Millar to wait by the door while he set up something at the fly-tying table. A minute or so later he called the older man to his side.

"Can you tell the difference, if any, in these three Jock Scots?" McGarr had stuck next to each other a completed fly that Nellie had made, the Jock Scot that he had taken from Niamh Goulding's fly box, and one of the Jock Scots that Ward had bought from Hank Stearns and, he assumed, had been tied by Jane Trowbridge.

Millar put on his spectacles and adjusted the stanchion of the large magnifying glass. He pointed to Jane Trowbridge's fly. "That's substantially different from the other two. It's a Freddy Riley." He meant it was a fly tied with feathers of birds that were sold in the food markets of the world and were readily available through fly-tackle catalogs.

Named after a man who developed the process of creating "nonexotic" flies, the Riley was a much cheaper, if not easier, fly to produce. Also, the method had helped to reduce the depredation of those rare wild birds from which traditional salmon-fly materials had come.

"Now, this fly here was tied by Nellie. It's a classic in every way—materials, character, and style."

By character, Millar meant its shape and general construction, which tended to be uniform in the work of an experienced fly-tier. By style, he meant the relative quantity of material that the tier tended to dress on a particular type of fly.

"Nellie liked a big, full Jock Scot. It's a beauty, isn't it?"

McGarr could only agree. The fly was a magnificent array of brilliant color and could be admired for its beauty, regardless of its fishing efficacy, which he imagined was also assured.

"This third fly, while expertly dressed, is a variant Jock Scot. You can see it isn't quite as full nor is it as round. Also, the tier has taken pains to expose the light gray roots at the base of the mallard wings. It's something that connoisseurs of Spey Flies attach great importance to, and sometimes the practice carries over to the tying of other flies. It's only a superstition, but many Scottish fishers believe that the bit of gray catches more fish. It's a rather common tic of some Scottish tiers.

"You can detect it better in these flies that Nellie was supposed to have tied the night ... " Millar moved to the incomplete flies, which were still attached to another cork rail. He trained the light on them, adding, "I only wished I'd had it in me to have examined the lot the afternoon we first came in here. After the wake.

"See here—adding the mallard wings was the last operation performed, since the tier was kept from proceeding for want of the jungle cock. See the gray roots in the mallard feathers?"

Every incomplete fly was showing light gray mallard roots.

"Nellie would never have done that. And then the tier was left-handed."

"The vise—here the lathe—may be turned, as though it had been used by a right-handed person, but all the implements are placed where the left hand can use them, while the materials are here to be held with the right. And if you'll notice the half hitches used to keep the various dressings in place? They're all just slightly to the left side of the Scot variant hook, as well as in the hooks of the incomplete flies. Instead of to the right side."

It was something that had escaped McGarr completely, he had been so intent on the flies themselves. Was Niamh Goulding left-handed? He did not know.

Millar straightened up and arched his back. When his eyes met McGarr's, he said, "Niamh Goulding?"

McGarr nodded. "It's time I had another wee talk with her."

# 21

# River Run

Hugh Ward had difficulty following the battered red Land Rover. Not only was Ardara's main street clogged with tourists, but also the town was getting ready to greet its Ulster Champion Gaelic football side. It was the first Donegal championship, the radio was reporting, in forty-two years, and a victory cavalcade was touring the larger county towns by auto.

When Ward saw the Rover top the hill by the church with him still down in front of the fly shop, he wished he had thought to get the use of a blue blinking light from the Garda barracks—the kind you could slap on the roof and plug into the cigarette lighter. But he had been distracted, to say the least.

And when Ward finally got to a bit of open road and sped the mile or so to the bridge over the Owenea, he wished he had also thought to arm himself. Having to fly into Scotland and then back to Northern Ireland, he had decided to eliminate the hassle that being an armed Irishman of any kind of description caused in the U.K. He had left his weapon back in Dublin Castle.

For at the bridge he found the Land Rover parked in the middle of the road and still idling, with Jane Trowbridge's bawling infant unattended in its car seat. Scanning the banks of the river, he caught sight of the mother walking quickly along the bank toward three figures that Ward recognized by the cowboy hat and a bright patch of red hair. The third was Niamh Goulding, who had reached her left hand into her wooden creel and now removed something shiny.

Seeing that too, Jane Trowbridge picked up speed, her long legs carrying her rapidly along the verge of the meadow. It was only then that Ward noticed she also had something in her right hand. But she kept it down by her side, as though to conceal it in the flare of her dress.

Ward vaulted the stile, sprinted down the metal walkway over the drainage ditch, and began running as fast as he could toward them.

For Ruth Bresnahan it had already been a difficult forty minutes in which she had been slowly, gradually, remorselessly sexually abused by an expert. She believed that Hank Stearns had already touched every part of her upper body but her nipples, and he would not be long sparing them.

All the while he kept talking. "No—the action of the rod must be kept from ten to two on the clock, so the line describes a gentle arc in the air without snapping. Anything more—you'll hang up in the brush behind us. Anything less, you'll make a poor cast and a worse presentation. *Big* salmon and *big* trout only give you one chance to offer your fly, and you have to place it before them with grace."

## Death on a Cold, Wild River

It all sounded professional with no heavy breathing, but at the same time, standing behind her to try to make her "rock" with him "all in one piece" with the two-handed rod, he squeezed and mauled and hugged her. At one point, he even patted her backside and said, "Good girl."

"Please, Hank," she protested, removing the hand. "You're distracting me. Can't we save that for later?"

Which was when a woman's voice said, "There'll be no bloody later for that bloody sod."

They both turned to see Niamh Goulding standing a few feet away on a knoll above the bank of the boiling river.

"Stand away from the bastard," she ordered, unsnapping the wooden creel and taking from it a bright silver handgun—something small, like a police off-duty revolver, Ruth judged. "I've no mind to kill you too, but I will, if I have to."

Stearns only gripped Ruth tighter and turned her toward the woman. "What's this all about, Niamh?"

"Ye ken right enough what it's about. Ye'r woman, the lanky bitch, just stole my fly shop from me with ye'r connivance. And ye'r money that ye stole from the safe. I should have figured ye'd plundered it afore I got there, when ye told the cop ye'd show him where Nellie kept the jungle cock. Ye'd taken it from the safe along with the money. And it was that you used to steal the shop from me."

"Nonsense, Niamh." Stearns laughed, but his voice was tight. "Jane comes from an old New England family. They've got plenty of money. She must have bought it with her inheritance. To spite me."

"Cock and shite. Ye're both in it tigither. She wouldna lived for months in that dank kip with ye'r bawling brood, if she came from money. And you only showed the cop the jungle cock to absolve ye'rself from having been in the place, after you killed Nellie out here. When you found the money in the safe, you decided you no longer needed a partner, and the way we set things up *you'd* go free. Poor thick Hal and thicker me would swing."

"What's this all about?" Ruth asked. "If you've something to settle, settle it without me." She tried to break Stearns's hold, but he held her fast. "Can't you put that thing down?" she pleaded with Goulding. "I want no part of this."

"There ye are, hiding behind a woman agin. It's what ye do best, but niver no more." She raised the barrel, and Bresnahan only caught a glimpse of another figure, who now appeared behind Goulding, before she pulled up her feet and—using the weight of her body—tumbled to the ground, breaking Stearns's hold on her waist.

A flurry of shots exploded around her—three short and sharp; and then the deafening roar of some large-caliber gun. Twice. Ruth rolled into the underbrush and, seeing a large rock, scrambled behind it. Her heart was in her mouth, her temples pounding. She glanced wildly around the treeless open barren behind her. There was no place to run or hide. She snatched up a stone and cocked her arm, only to hear a deeper woman's voice say, "Let me go, we can still save my husband."

Hugh Ward had arrived at the scene a half-step too late. When he saw Jane Trowbridge raise the weapon in her right hand, he lowered his shoulders and lunged to tackle her.

But hafting the gun—some large-caliber automatic—in both hands in a practiced manner, Trowbridge squeezed off one shot, then swung the barrel, and fired again.

Ward's shoulder struck her just below the knees, and she fell roughly into the deep grass on the bank of the river. Ward scrambled up and stomped her wrist, then pried the gun from her grasp.

Pivoting in a crouch, he pointed the barrel at the other person he had seen with a weapon. But she was half in the river, eyes open, water streaming over her head. There was a large hole gushing blood from her chest. Left side, an inch from her sternum, right through her heart.

The cowboy? Ward caught sight of his hat being tossed by the current, maybe a hundred yards downstream. Followed by Stearns himself, whose face appeared now and then as he was catapulted through the rapids.

"He's in the river! He's *in* the river!" Ward shouted to McGarr, whom he could now see at the bridge where a number of cars were now stopped, people getting out to gawk.

Ruthie. She now stepped out from behind a large boulder.

"You all right?"

She nodded. "And you?"

Ward pointed to the silver handgun, which was resting in the mud by the feet of the dead woman, before turning to sprint down the river bank after Stearns.

The Trowbridge woman was picking herself up.

Ruth retrieved Niamh Goulding's silver automatic, which she tucked under the belt of her fishing trousers. She then turned her attention to Goulding herself, whose blond hair was streaming in the current. The wooden creel bobbed several yards downstream, its strap snagged around her neck.

"Don't move," Ruth said to the American woman, bending to pull Niamh Goulding's corpse up onto the riverbank.

"I've got to get back to my baby." She was fitting on her wide sun hat, as though nothing had happened.

Hank Stearns was dead when McGarr and Ward pulled him from the Owenea. He had a small-caliber wound in one shoulder, but a large black hole right in the center of his forehead.

Looking down at her dead husband, with his baby now in her arms, Jane Trowbridge said, "I must have missed her. She fired first and would have killed us all, like she killed Nellie Millar. This woman is my witness." She meant Ruth.

Trowbridge's expensive shoes were back on her feet, the wide-brimmed sun hat neatly on her head. "I must return to my other children. The baby-sitter will be worried."

# PART V

*An rud is annamh is iontach.*
  (An Irish saying: What's seldom is wonderful.)

# 22

# Moonlight and Ruses

There is a hill just beyond the Diamond in the center of Ardara that can be most private. It also enjoys one of the finest views in all of Ireland, especially on a summer night under a clear, storm-scoured sky.

Some hours later, shortly after sundown, Hugh Ward and Ruth Bresnahan appeared in one of the walled pastures on the hilltop, carrying a number of items that Ward had purchased in the village. While Ward deployed his impedimenta, Bresnahan looked down on the village, which was lit brilliantly now in preparation for the arrival of its victorious football side. Bands had already gathered from Donegal Town, Dungloe, and Killybegs, and the auto cavalcade of victorious heroes was said to be on its way.

Ruth raised her eyes. Under the chalky waning moon, the gentle rolling hills, farmhouses, and white sand beaches of Loughros Point—which divided the broad bay—looked nearly achromatic, like a negative image in photography or a kind of silver dreamscape. Farther still was the dark imminence of Slieve Tooey, its gently curving crest spangled with an array of bright stars. And overhead? Well—there the stars were so multiform, complex, and deep that staring at them made Ruth rather giddy. She glanced back at Ward.

He had spread the double-width sleeping bag out before a tramcock of hay, against which they might rest their backs for chat, if needed, and he had opened one of two bottles of Sauternes (she liked things sweet). Also arrayed was a variety of snacks, in case they got the munchies *after*, as they sometimes had of old. Had he forgotten anything? Not that he could think of. Even nature was cooperating: a warm, gentle breeze was wafting in from the east, and the celebration in the village was providing just the right amount of "white noise" to make the setting what Ward considered a bucolic ideal. That is, as accommodating as the country could ever be for him.

He turned to Ruth, who would be the centerpiece of his . . . arrangement.

"Isn't this a bit hackneyed? Not to say dangerous. Already today one man tried to mash me on the banks of a river, and look what happened to him. Here you are on a hilltop."

"Ah, but he failed to provide the magic elixir." Ward held up the open bottle.

"What is it?" Bresnahan nevertheless sat and picked up one of the stemmed glasses. "A dram from the fabled pool of life?"

"Into which drop nuts from five yew trees—representing the five kingdoms of ancient Ireland—and are et by the Salmon, thereby giving him the knowledge that he then swims to Fionn, via the Druid Cyclops? You must have been speaking with Noreen. She was running on and on about that lot over dinner."

"No, after Fionn it's the *Blind* Druid Cyclops. He has a smoldering brand sticking from his eye. Better than the barb of salmon fly. I nearly blinded meself learning to cast this afternoon. To say nothing of that poor, dead, murderer, God rest his greedy, conniving, woman-molesting soul."

Ward did not like the tenor of that remark, woman-molesting being very much on his mind. "Noreen even had a book about it that she borrowed from the library in Donegal Town," he went on. "Proof 'resonantly mythological,' said she, 'that the solution to Nellie Millar's murder lay all along in the salmon flies that Peter and Nellie's father found in the fly shop. You know, in the way that the Salmon of All Knowledge ate the nuts from the yew trees, you substitute—"

" 'In this context,' " Ruth said, holding up a finger and staring down at it gravely the way Noreen always did when making a crucial point.

" 'Consubstantial yew nuts, that is, salmon flies. And there you have it.' "

They both laughed, and Ward filled their glasses. "Isn't this like old times?"

"You mean, laughing *at* Noreen?"

"No, *with* Noreen. Remember, the Chief is again—"

"THE CHIEF!" they said together, Ward adding, "and not even a polite titter at her expense, unless you desire to feel the weight of his or—worse—*her* profoundly knowledge-able tongue."

"Pity our poor wits, but she's beautiful and charming, so she is," Ruth put in, defending both her friend and her gender.

"I know one man who thinks so," said Ward.

"Speaking of which"—Bresnahan turned her face to him—"can you credit the fact that I'm still alive, and here you sit? With me? Still?"

Ward nearly put down his glass, so that he'd have both hands free for mashing.

But Ruth went on. "Explain to me now, before you anticipate yourself, the scenario leading up to Nellie Millar's death. You know, how Stearns and Goulding 'worked' the crime. This is lovely wine."

Ward coughed; he hoped it was the modifier exactly.

"Where'd you get it, in town?" She picked up the bottle, before he could pull it away from her, and she saw the Dublin Airport sticker on the side. "Rather sure of yourself, weren't you? Or were you intending the elixir for some other maiden-of-the-stream? Tell me—did you and the Chief set the whole thing up, ringing me in Kerry with the assignment that *only I* could handle?"

"Not a'tall, not a'tall," Ward replied in his worst Dublin accent, which was what McGarr spoke. "Me mudder's got a taste for the shtuff, but I figger she can wait."

"Your mudder doesn't drink, as I remember her. Begin with the scenario, and then ramble on to your plot."

Ward eased his back into the soft, fragrant hay and tucked a hand behind his head. He stared up at the moon. "Well—Niamh Goulding was right about Stearns, whom I, for one, can understand completely."

"How so?" Bresnahan eased herself down beside him and followed his gaze to the moon. She took his free hand.

"Stearns was a man who believed he could not actualize himself without the . . . assistance of woman, and he was desperate because of his failed former career as a university don and the difficulty of breaking into something like sports angling as a profession. Having been—and continuing to be—a victim of him herself, his wife, Jane Trowbridge, knew he was a user of women. But she also knew that if he was ever going to support her and their children,

Stearns would probably be able to do it most easily *through* other women."

"Literally. So she went along with his philandering."

"Or dysfunctional behavior."

"Where'd you get a word like that?"

"I've had plenty of time to read the past nine months."

"As long as you weren't being 'tutored' by Carla Jung. You know, on the couch."

"I'd be freudened of her father."

"So?"

"So, Nellie Millar seemed perfect for Stearns. She was an older, still attractive woman who was successful and well respected internationally in the profession he was trying to enter. Also, she was alone and vulnerable. He began preying upon those vulnerabilities—her need of companionship, somebody to keep her warm of a night, somebody to share her experiences on streams, rivers, and lakes. Every couple needs something beyond the odd tumble to keep them together." Ward moved closer to Bresnahan.

"Like murder?" she asked.

"Well—serious crime. It seems to work for the McGarrs."

"Yes, but their togetherness is based on serious *intellectualized* crime."

When they stopped laughing, Ward went on. "But it was plain from Nellie's diary entries, from what the Chief learned from her father, and even from what Stearns said himself, that he was just a fling for her. She would never make him—or anybody—a partner."

"Why *should* she have?" Ruth inquired indignantly. "Hadn't she defined her business as that of one woman offering other mainly independent women the opportunity of learning about a solitary sport *without* the aid or assis-

tance or necessity of men? When I think of how that ...
louse—"

"*Dead* louse."

"Felicitously *dead* louse manhandled me this afternoon!"

"I'm happy to learn fly-fishing's not for you," Ward said,
in order to turn the topic from manhandling and lice, dead
or otherwise.

"It's cruel."

"To the fish?"

"I was thinking more of the women who have to learn
all that ten-to-two-on-the-clock, fly-casting carry-on and,
you know, compete with men who've been doing it since
they were lads."

"That was just Nellie's point. It's an art, not a science
or competition to see who can catch the most fish. You
practice it on your own, for yourself, and *with* nature.
Didn't you read all those sayings she tacked up around her
shop? Only when she was goaded by Stearns and Goulding—they wrote those letters that were sent to *Eire Rod
and Reel* condemning her—did she fish *for* fish, and she
ended up paying."

"With her life." Ruth sipped from her glass. "Which
brings us to Shevlin."

"A dupe. They set him up too—informing the marine
fishing authorities about his illegal drift-netting and making it seem like it was Nellie, who *had* been keeping tabs
on Shevlin, mind. But nothing else."

"Then Niamh Goulding 'befriended' Shevlin," said
Ruth.

"With friends like that, you don't need enemas. How's
your wine?"

"She probably bought him drinks too."

"Not wine, I'd hazard. Where was I?"

"Shevlin and his knife, which Stearns used to slit the waders."

"Ah, yes—they'd need something more tangible than the mere hatred of a convicted illegal drift-netter-turned-poacher who was probably out on the river every night salmon were running."

"Physical evidence, since—"

"Murderers always try too hard," they said together, Ruth adding, "Thank you, Chief."

"Which was not that hard to arrange, with Shevlin probably half-seas-over and browned-off."

"Sounds like an omelet. But why didn't they just let her drown and be done with it? Niamh Goulding could have bought the house and fly shop and taken Stearns on as her partner, and so forth."

"Because Stearns obviously insisted that he not be known to have been the last person to be seen with Nellie before her death. You know, him having made the cut in the waders. If the cut was found, he wanted it said that he had left her on the river still very much alive and still fishing. Also, he wanted some others to think they saw Nellie tying flies in her shop, *after* he was seen in Nancy's Pub.

"Remember, not a few people, including her father, knew that he'd been haunting Nellie for over a year, lusting after her business."

"Can you lust after business?" Ruth asked. "Or does one lust after *the* business?"

"That's different and will come later, I promise. Haunting her, as he did, it must have occurred to him that the fly shop was not only an excellent business, but also that a good amount of her revenue was not being recorded in the books. Maybe he suspected that she was turning it into cash. Or maybe he just saw her at the safe, getting out some jungle cock."

"What an appellation!"

"I won't touch that."

"I won't you, if you do."

"Let the record show that she will, since I won't. And since it was Stearns who must also have known where Nellie kept her keys at home."

"And he who entered the shop first after her death."

"And only he who could have done the *ground* work, ahem, to come up with the combination to the safe."

"Then it could only be he who opened the safe *before* Niamh Goulding showed up to play Nellie at the fly-tying vise."

"Not a stupid man, a Ph.D. scientist—analytical in spite of his...cowboy drag that probably would not 'carry' in his own country, where he'd be revealed as a fraud from industrial Ohio—he seized upon the opportunity to use the great bomb of money that he discovered in the safe—"

"More than he could have dreamed."

"To buy the fly shop and its excellent catalog business for himself."

"He'd had enough of nonpartnership, and Niamh Goulding was no prize."

"Also there was his nonwife and nonfamily."

"How many degrees of denial was this man in?"

"Countless. So he glommed the money and all hackles but one of jungle cock—a nice touch that, what? And in so doing he set Niamh Goulding up. He then let her into the shop and went on his way."

"Which was back to Nellie's for her new Rover, which he drove out to the car park by the bridge. He parked and locked it, as though she herself had returned from town in it to fish."

"Exactly. Meanwhile, Shevlin was in Ardara, selling his own poached fish."

"Fish that had been poached," Ruth corrected. "No, that's not quite right either. His poachings."

"Better. Selling his poachings in town. Noting a light on in the fly shop, he chanced to look in and see a woman at the fly-tying vise whom he knew could not be Nellie Millar, since not long before he had watched her drown. He must have waited until she left the shop and caught her coming out. It led to a few hundred quid and a job in Garmouth, Scotland. Later, of course, he'd *touch* her for more, but it was a start. Shevlin is no prize.

"What he didn't know was that his knife, which he had lost in Goulding's room at the Nesbitt Arms sometime before, was actually the murder weapon, so to speak."

"And he was to be Stearns's and Goulding's—or at least Goulding's—patsy, if they required one."

"Well—maybe he had an inkling of that, which is why he spoke to the Chief at the bridge."

"So, when did the Stearns-Goulding partnership first start breaking up?" Ruth asked.

"When Stearns realized the Chief was on to something in the shop, and he saw the opportunity of incriminating Goulding at no loss to himself."

"In the pub when the Chief asked him about the jungle cock. There's that phrase again."

Ward nodded. "Delightful as it is. Niamh Goulding then panicked and decided to surrender the knife—Shevlin's knife—to McGarr, thereby passing off the most damaging evidence. Shevlin's absconding to Scotland, of course, would make him seem all the more guilty, and there he was—already a convicted criminal, with his motive for wanting Nellie Millar dead very much a matter of public record."

Said Ruth, "Niamh Goulding must have felt secure enough. *She* hadn't personally slit the waders or been present out on the river to watch Nellie drown. At most she had written some anonymous letters and tied a few salmon flies."

"And there we have it, crime complete. Apart from Stearns's biggest mistake, which was what?"

"If you're trying to get me to say, trusting women, I won't."

"No—*marrying*, or at least having three children by a woman who was an *actual* cowgirl from Montana and could shoot straight."

"But Stearns said she was from New England, I heard him."

"And he said a lot of other tripe, too, for which he paid. That bullet was no accident."

"And you're no jury. A decent barrister will make Jane Trowbridge look like more of a victim than Nellie Millar. She'll even contend that Trowbridge did not know where the money came from, that Stearns set her up, that Trowbridge was only trying to protect him—as she said, and I witnessed—the father of her children. I wouldn't be a bit surprised if she gets to keep the fly shop, given the impossibility of proving the money actually came from Nellie's safe."

"And a stray bullet just happened to strike him right between the eyes. Did you check the position of the entry wound? It looked like the spot the priest gives you in church on Ash Wednesday. I bet an investigation would prove that she's some sort of dab shot. A champion markswoman.

*Death on a Cold, Wild River*

"By the by, what's this *she* stuff. Don't tell me living down in Kerry has turned you into a libber."

Ruth did not know what he meant.

"She, the barrister."

"I was just keeping the recapitulation balanced. But now that you mention it, there can't be many women barristers about."

"Because they can only attract clients from half the population."

Ruth waited.

"Women are too wise, they don't trust them."

"I wonder—maybe that would be a good thing for me to get into."

"Nonsense, it would take years—university, exams, practice, and so forth."

"I've got time. And money from me da now."

"You mean, you're not planning to come back to The Squad?"

"How could I? I've been away for nine months. If I tried, personnel would probably send me out someplace like this. You know, to make an example of me. Being a woman and all."

"But you never left."

"I *resigned*."

"Ah, hell—if that's all you're worried about, I tore that bastard up and put you on sympathetic leave. Because of your father. I've got a drawerful of pay packets back in Dublin, waiting for you."

"You're coddin'."

Not yet, Ward thought, but soon. "More wine?"

"Nah—I've had enough." Ruth put the glass aside and eased herself down into the soft down bag. "There's nothing like a good solution to warm a body up." She twined her fingers behind her head. "And now for the plot."

"Which plot?"

"You and the Chief? I want you to tell me how much you missed me, and if you mention your pocket, I'm out of here."

"Well"—Ward glanced down at his trousers—"what form should my confession take?"

"Oh, I don't know. You're the one with the devious mind who arranged all of this. Use your imagination."

# 23

# Fionn-land

With a klieg light and binoculars, Peter McGarr might have seen Bresnahan and Ward up in the pasture above Ardara. He was standing before the windows of his suite in the Nesbitt Arms Hotel, looking down at the spectacle unfolding in 'the Diamond' below him. Across the open area, a large lorry with a portable stage had been erected and a public-address system rigged. Now an assortment of bands marched by.

The best, at least to his untutored ear, was St. Catherine's of Killybegs, which featured fourteen keyboard accordions, a like number of xylophones, many tambourines, and a few excellent drums. The combined sound was strange—something like Cajun music—and delivered in a confident, cheerful manner that left McGarr in a kind of awe at its brashness. In front were some not-so-wee lassies with good legs, who were dressed, like the others, in red-white and gold marching uniforms.

Stopping in front of the stage, they suddenly abandoned

their martial rectitude, and danced wildly but in synch to songs like "The Twist" and "Tequila."

"Do they drink tequila in New Orleans?" McGarr asked Noreen, who had installed herself in the largest armchair to read the book on Irish myth that she had borrowed from the Donegal Town library.

"What's tequila?" Maddie asked; she was standing by McGarr's side and also looking down on the parade. "I want to be a majorette."

"I suspect they drink everything there is in New Orleans," Noreen replied without looking up from the book.

Which sounded right to McGarr, and he was suddenly in need of a drink. But not tequila.

When the music stopped, a number of local officials advanced on the microphone and delivered encomiums to the prodigious feat (feet?) of pediform, manual, and only occasionally fistic excellence that Donegal men had demonstrated in their victory in the Ulster final. Still the cavalcade of actual heroes was not in sight, and more than a few of the speakers guessed that the stalwart lads might be having "a drop or two" forced on them as made their way toward Ardara.

When finally they arrived and mounted the stage to the uproarious approval of all, an older man and former football notable introduced the younger man who had scored the winning tally, then said, "Today, when the chips were down, Niall passed the ball off to Mick, who passed it to Dermot, who pass it to this lad here, Gabriel. Who *scored*! Now, that to me is greatness!"

The crowd roared, in spite of the message.

When Gabriel stepped to the microphone, all he could manage after the wetting he had obviously suffered over the last several days was, "I want to thank yez for all turning up. Yous got behind us, and we did the business."

The crowd was beside itself and virtually mugged its heroes, rushing up on stage. Even younger lads were waving exercise books, looking for autographs.

"What are they doing, Daddy?" Maddie asked.

It was a good question, a fair question, but how to answer it and be understood by a three-year-old?

What McGarr was seeing before him was community. It was not *his* community, since as a Dubliner he no longer had anything so definite, but community was rare in this day and age. It did not matter what was said or by whom, what mattered was that the people below him were expressing their togetherness and what their lads from this barren, excruciatingly beautiful place had done in their name. It was little really, but since this was a community that had been under constant siege for over three hundred years, because of the necessity of emigration, any victory was sweet.

Equally apparent, on the other hand, was that Donegal was fertile ground for myth—like that of their victorious football team whose exploits would be praised, glorified, and undoubtedly exaggerated for the decades it might take to win the Ulster Cup again. McGarr thought of how immediate the adventure of Finn MacCool and the Salmon of All Knowledge had been to the old crone in the churchyard by Nellie's grave. She had spoken of it in the present tense, as though Finn's adventure in the cave had only just occurred.

A quick, unfair judgment of the footballers on the platform stage would have them merely a gang of thugs and toughs. Like Finn's boys had undoubtedly been, they were a young, strong, evidently quick lot, ready with feet, fists, and heads should anybody challenge their manhood. But as well, a fair few of them might be lawyers or doctors, or, *better*, people who knew themselves as creatures of this society and this land. And that, after all, was something invaluable, and perhaps what had attracted Nellie Millar to this place.

To Maddie, McGarr said, "They're celebrating being together."

Of Noreen, he asked, "Was Finn MacCool an actual person or was he . . . mythological?"

"Neither. He was a culture hero. He—or somebody like him—probably existed, but whether deified or not, a culture hero can be distinguished from other cult figures by the purposeful and useful things he or she brings to the people. For instance, Prometheus, who brought fire to man, is a culture hero. Fire is light. Light is knowledge. Like—"

"Finn," said McGarr.

"Exactly. Fionn was the center of an immense cycle of narratives, so it says here." She held up the book. "But it's the Promethean character of Fionn that makes him a culture hero, and one of the reasons—I should imagine— that Joyce appropriated the Fionn myth for his *Wake*."

"*Finn-agains Wake*," McGarr said to himself, realizing for the first time the connection. And there he thought he was too old or too . . . corrupted to learn.

"Know what?" Noreen asked.

Staring down at the moil below him, McGarr did not have a clue, apart from the fact that he needed to join them. For a drink. For community.

"If I had read this book before I got here, I could have told you who it was who"—for Maddie's sake she elided the word *murdered*—murdered "Nellie the moment I got here."

With baleful brow, McGarr turned to her. "How?"

"Because a character in the Fionn myths is actually named Niamh. Can you believe it?"

McGarr would, because it was written, undoubtedly after much painful research.

"She was an old, blind hag, grasping, greedy, and murderous, who could transform herself into anything she wanted, including a beautiful woman. At will."

McGarr glanced at the door, where he could escape. Would he have to don a fleece? "But your knowing that couldn't have determined that *this* Niamh participated in the"—he coughed—"of Nellie Millar."

"But so much else was in place. You know, Nellie as a fisher. For salmon. Nellie the white-capped, independent, and daring one."

McGarr turned for the door. "Remind me to consult myth the next time we're in these parts. Officially."

Maddie ran to him. "Don't you want to play *Caspar the Friendly Ghost*?" It was a video that fascinated her.

"That's *Oscar*, if you want to keep it right," said Noreen. "Originally. Whoever transformed the myth got the name wrong."

"When I get back," McGarr nearly said "baby," but it was a term that Maddie no longer accepted. "When I get back."

McGarr had yet to mourn the passing of Nellie Millar in Finn—or Fionn—style, but now he would.

And could.